Praise 1

The characters and [...] . It's a story of greed, goodn[...] ackest of souls with the use of Paranormal and Horror. She also illustrates the goodness, light, and power of people with generous souls. The interaction between the characters is brilliant. I loved the story line, felt as though I knew the characters and the writing really impressed me. This novel brilliantly portrays what Karma really is.
~Kathleen Ball

The Turn of the Karmic Wheel is truly a story to take to heart. It cautions us against being self-centered, hateful, and prone to venial sins. We all have choices in this life and it's up to us to make the best of what we're given. If we follow the Golden rule, we can reap the rewards of kindness, love, and reciprocity in this life. Each character's story seems at first to be a separate entity, yet as we move along in the book, we are shown that everyone in the world is connected to one another. Yet, we can all lose sight of that message and let darkness seep into our souls. The characters are well-developed and each has flaws - no one is entirely good or entirely evil. A beautiful blend of mysticism and spirituality, Ms. Brinkman has written an unforgettable and moving tale which will make you re-evaluate your own actions.
~Star@ The Bibliophilic Book Blog

This book begins by introducing the readers to a diverse group of characters at first they seem to have no connection except they all live in the same town. As the plot develops the reader watches as their lives cross paths. The main characters are average everyday people. Angela, Karman and Euclid are the "good" people. The bad people are Joshua, Monty and Rosie. Their sins are gluttony, covetousness and disregard for others. The sins are about to catch up with the bad guys. Some of the things that happen to them will turn your stomach. (You just might want to check out your facial cream and toothpaste before using it.) There were visions, voices and odd happenings in the town.

The Turn of the Karmic Wheel takes a look at karma, a more frightening look. The premise of this book is that we all have decisions to make and each decision has consequences. There is a depth to the plot... Author Monica Brinkman ... has created a unique plot and vibrant characters. The genre is a cross between thriller and horror... I look forward to reading the next one.
~ Anne Boeling

A HUNTING WE WILL GO

"Get 'em good, get 'em right, get 'em day, or get 'em night," Euclid mumbled, a wide smirk spreading across his fifty-nine-year-old face. No one knew the deep secrets he hid inside his head and he aimed to keep it that way. "Me a friend, me a fool, me is ugly as a ghoul," whispered Euclid, then broke out in a roar of laughter edged with a bit of insanity.

Morning clouds opened, producing fine drops of rain upon the ground. Euclid wiped the drizzle from his face as he entered McFarland's Sporting Goods Store. He removed the cap from his head, revealing tufts of thinning gray-and-brown hair, which he brushed to one side with a sweep of his hand.

Forty-eight-year-old Henry Joseph McFarland stood behind the counter and greeted Euclid with a cheery "Good morning, Brother Euclid. What brings you here on this cold and dreary day?"

Henry was what the women in Raleigh would call 'a catch indeed'. He stood six foot five inches tall, with large hazel eyes and sandy, blonde curly hair he now wore cropped to his head. The weekly gym workouts kept his body firm and well-muscled, though vanity was not part of Henry's makeup. At his age, the doc said he required physical activity to keep the 'old ticker' going strong, so he opted for the gym. It worked into his schedule just fine.

"I am lookin' for, er, a hunting rifle," Euclid said as he neared Henry, the smirk still on his face.

"Well, what kind of game you after," Harry inquired. "Turkey?

Beaver? Deer? I got the best firearm for them all."

"I can tell you it's big, it's mean, and it gets what it wants."

"Are you seeking dual action for both game and bird?"

After pondering the question a moment, Euclid responded, "If it will do the job, sure."

"Hmm, well, your best bet is a 243 Winchester Super Short Magnum. Not only is it accurate and versatile, it's easy to use and get's the game. I'll grab one out of the back and see if it's to your liking," Harry stated as he walked toward the warehouse door.

A few moments later Harry returned to the counter with rifle in hand."I have a great deal on this Winchester rifle right now. It's going for—"

"I'll take it," Euclid said, as he cut off Harry's offer. Excitedly, he continued, "Wrap it up. Oh, and I got a few extra bucks for ya if you speed up the legal stuff. Can ya do this for me, Harry? I would be much obliged."

Looking directly into Euclid's eager eyes, Harry responded, "Sure, it's a deal!" He never was one to look a gift horse in the mouth, but couldn't bring himself to take advantage of what seemed a very desperate man. Probably needed food on the table as soon as possible. Turkey season would end shortly, but there was still enough time to tag a few of them. No, he couldn't take one more cent than the asking price.

Gesturing by a wave of his left hand to follow him, Harry said, "I'll have none of that, my friend. Come on over to the counter and we'll fill out the documents the state and government require."

"Appreciate your help, Harry, knew I could depend on ya. 'Bout time I fended for myself."

"Not a bad idea," Harry answered. "You'll need a hunting license, and you might think of getting a fishing license soon. As I said, I'm giving you a decent price. And if I can help you with some tips on hunting techniques, you let me know. Those wild turkeys can be tricky to snare."

"Just may take ya up on that offer, Harry. Again, I'm much obliged," Euclid responded.

After completing the mass of paperwork, Euclid extended his arm, gave Harry a strong handshake, nodded his head and stated, "Will be callin' ya soon."

"You'll be able to pick up the rifle tomorrow. Give me a call mid-morning. Should be cleared and ready to go by that time."

Euclid nodded and exited the store.

Harry had owned his shop for many years, seen some come in and go out in a sea of police gunfire, but, hell, he couldn't worry about every customer who purchased a weapon. Fact was, he had given up trying to figure out man's nature years ago. Course, Euclid wasn't one to carry arms of any sort. He didn't remember him ever going hunting or even showing interest in the sport. Perhaps now that he was alone in life, with much time on his hands, he had decided to take it up and save some money by providing his own meat for the table. In any event, Harry knew Euclid to be a solid citizen of Raleigh, a man with a pure heart. Yes, he was a good man and a great friend.

Harry went to the window and watched his friend walk down the street. He wondered if he should be concerned. For some reason, he felt a bit of uneasiness; just couldn't put his finger on the why or wherefore. Aw, hell, he reasoned, it ain't none of my business.

Yet there was something eating at his mind, a voice telling him to go no further with this transaction. It was a gut feeling he couldn't shake, a feeling that his friend and neighbor of over 30 years was not 'quite right'. There was definitely something 'off the scale' about Euclid today.

A vivid image entered his mind. A vision so unfathomable he had to let it go.

Harry shivered as he moved to slowly close the store's door, continuing to watch the retreating figure kicking stones along the road, unable to shake his feelings of dread.

The Wheel's Final Turn

Monica M. Brinkman

The Wheel's Final Turn
Copyright © 2015 by Monica M. Brinkman

All rights reserved. No part of this book may be reproduced or transmitted in any form or by any means without written permission of the author and publisher.

This is a work of fiction. Any resemblance to real people, living or dead, is purely coincidental. While certain locations are real, fictional liberties have been taken with certain aspects of their geography and history.

ISBN: 978-09907158-8-7
Library of Congress Control Number: 2015940565

Cover design by All Things That Matter Press.

I wish to dedicate this book to my husband, Richard Brinkman.

Without his understanding, encouragement and patience,
I doubt I would have made it to the last chapter and
the ultimate end of the story.

Acknowledgments

I must acknowledge my editor, Deb Harris, and publisher, All Things That Matter Press, who has been there no matter how silly a question I might present to them or how often I made inquiries. Deb's editing skills are perfection, and, without her, this story would not have made it to the light of day.

Prologue

FOREWARNED

Angela sat still and silent, arms to her side and legs placed firmly on the ground. The musky odor of the dank room filled her nostrils as she took a deep breath and slowly exhaled. Her long blonde hair, secured in a ponytail, cascaded down the back of the worn Adirondack chair; her green eyes were shut tight as she allowed the music to enter her mind. The wondrous sound encased her, caressing her body and embracing her soul. She was lost in an existence of pure beauty and exquisite motion and wonderment.

She bolted upright, her euphoria interrupted, arms tense, hands tightly grasping the sides of the chair. A Mephistophelian darkness had shown its face as a repulsive melody filled her ears. Angela blinked her eyes once, then again, to rid herself of the evil that had disturbed her peace and tranquility. She shuddered, trembling in apprehension of what she knew was to occur—to her, to friends, to family and, perhaps, ultimately to humanity.

PART I

ACCEPTANCE

From the start of time, they questioned all
the reason for man's protocol
Each side speaking their own truth
configured to gain fortitude
among the mass of peers
Essence baffling the mind
of kings, presidents, seers

~Monica M. Brinkman, 2014

Chapter One
Governor Jared Williams

It was a chilly, dismal day, perfect for staying snuggled up in a warm, cozy thick blanket away from the outside world.

Jared Williams sat behind his rich antique mahogany desk, tipped his brown Italian leather chair backward, and let out an extended sigh. He gazed at the stack of letters piled in front of him, knowing it was his duty to go through them and respond, but the truth was he didn't feel up to the task. He thought he'd go out of his frigging mind if he had to read one more letter from some out of work wacko, or yet another permanently disabled firefighter, or recently terminated educator. The public, unsophisticated in the reality of political workings, actually thought their elected servants gave a damn about their pathetic little lives. With a sweep of his right hand, he sent the letters flying across the desk and into the garbage container. A few missed their target and ended up on the plush beige carpet. He left them for Environmental Services to tend to.

God, he was bored. It was Friday afternoon and most of the staff had left around noon. He could hear the faint click, click, click of the computer keyboard through his partially open door as his secretary, Yolanda Mendez, typed the final draft of the speech he would be giving tomorrow night for the California Small Business Association. *Hope it's a crowd pleaser* crossed his mind, only to be replaced by a vision of Yolanda's perky young breasts rubbing against her crisp white cotton blouse. He imagined her pouty full lips sucking the breath out of him, his hands caressing her full, perfectly formed buttocks. She was what he called a hot tamale, pure one hundred percent Mexican heritage with thick black hair, clear light brown skin, and crescent shaped deep brown eyes surrounded by dense long eyelashes. A groan of passion, quickly stifled, accompanied the broad smile that filled his face as he allowed himself to be swept away in his delightful daydream.

***

Jared kept himself in good physical condition. He watched what he ate and visited the local gym at least four times a week. His dark brown hair, tinted with streaks of grey at the temples and through his sideburns, only accentuated the blueness of his eyes. He stood an even six feet tall, and possessed the sexual endurance of a much younger man. Too bad

Elaine, his wife of eighteen years, seemed not to appreciate these qualities.

Jared scooted his chair back, propped his long legs onto the desk and crossed them at the ankles. Memories of their beginning seeped into his thoughts as he stared toward the ceiling. Elaine, she of the long auburn hair, soft skin the color of freshly churned milk, and large, oval-shaped russet eyes. At one time, he'd worshipped her. He thought he'd found the girl of his dreams. She was of good breeding and above-average intelligence. He felt like the luckiest man alive when she accepted his proposal of marriage. His family was upper middle-class while she belonged to the social class of servants, butlers, and coddling. Her father was a well-known prosecuting attorney turned County Judge.

Elaine was an only child, spoiled by her father, Judge Albert Ponte, who had made it clear he would not easily give up the protective web of security or power of control he'd so carefully placed around his beloved child. Jared had expected a long, drawn out lecture or interrogation from the old geezer. To his surprise, the normally solemn Albert smiled and welcomed him to the family, extended his arm and offered a firm handshake in approval of their upcoming nuptials.

For the first few years, life was grand as they experienced marital bliss both in and out of the bedroom. His father-in-law generously agreed to take Jared, fluent in several foreign dialects, on as a court interpreter while he finished law school. Elaine busied herself attending social functions, shopping at the finest stores, and maintaining her stunning looks.

Jared's life changed dramatically the day he and Elaine discussed starting a family. He was shocked when Elaine reeled back from his touch, a look of revulsion upon her face at the mere mention of offspring. Soon Jared realized his catch was nothing less than the ultimate booby prize, preferring to indulge her own vanity rather than raise a family.

Elaine required constant and consistent pampering. Everything centered on *her* needs, *her* wants, and *her* world. Shortly after his suggestion that they start a family, she moved his belongings into the bedroom on the second floor. He was reduced to pleading and begging for even a moment of sexual pleasure. Then he discovered the magic of plastic. A few swipes of the credit card, a new dress, a pair of shoes, and she'd turn into a smooth operator, fulfilling her wifely duties with the expertise of an experienced sexual therapist—with one unbreakable rule: protection. Their marriage became more like a business contract than a relationship, one which he tired of within a few years. Elaine was tolerant of his sexual romps outside of their marriage—as long as he kept the money pouring in.

The buzzer of the intercom interrupted his reminiscing.

"Governor, Andrew Filbert is on line one. Should I put the call through?"

"Not now, Yolanda. Take a message."

Hell, no, that's all I need today, a lengthy conversation with the treasurer on balancing the budget. It was bad enough he'd had to work out of this crappy office since they closed the governor's mansion again, claiming the additional repairs it needed would be too much of a burden on the taxpayers. He wanted the prominence having his office there would bring, but those damn Democrats had ruined any chance of that ever happening.

Jared pressed the intercom button for Yolanda.

"Yes, sir?"

"Yolanda, please hold all calls for the rest of the day. And bring me that draft as soon as you finish typing it up. I want to look polished tomorrow night."

"Yes, sir, right away."

He loved hearing Yolanda's voice. It was sweet and clear with a husky undertone. She was one of the few bright spots of each workday.

Jared pulled his chair closer to the desk, sat upright, awaiting the arrival of his speech. He preferred paper in his hand rather than looking at a computer screen. It was time to concentrate on memorizing what he would say. As governor of the State of California, he felt it his duty to be fully prepared, even as he recognized it would be yet another boring speech full of half-truths and even outright lies.

He'd learned early in the game that his political status rested with the large corporations who financed the majority of his campaign and those of his constituents. The reality was that no one in the state was overly concerned with the failure of small business. There was no American Dream anymore.

Jared wondered how he could have been so naïve in his youth. He'd wanted to change the world. And, even more idiotic, believed he was the man to do it. He shook his head, thinking back to the time when he had decency and morals, when he genuinely felt it possible to share the glorious wealth and resources of his country. Back then, he was positive that by going into law, and later politics, he would realize his dreams.

***

Jared's first love had been music. His Uncle George had been lead guitarist with the well-known Academy Fools band, most famous during the early '70s. He'd first heard Uncle George play Hunger Among the Multitude, an interpretation of chords, beginning slow, soft, and pure, ending in the climatic crescendo of masterly fingered guitar movements embodying the emotions of pain, despondency, and hopelessness the song's words portrayed.

Jared's secret ambition had been to master the guitar and one day become as brilliant and famous a player as his uncle. He'd once made the mistake of sharing this dream with his father. Senior's reaction would have led a casual observer to think his son had admitted to pursuing a life of crime. His father's face scrunched, eyes slit with anger as he placed his large hands on Jared's shoulders and swept him to his feet, shouting, "Hear me loud and clear, son. I will never condone my flesh and blood taking up the music profession. It's immoral, degrading, and disgusting. Cheap women, drugs. I won't have it."

"But, Dad, I love music. It is not degrading or immoral."

A sharp slap stung his face and he boy relied on every ounce of inner strength he had to hold back the tears of pain and hurt.

"I will *not* hear one more word about it, do you understand me?"

"Yes, sir."

At nine years of age, Jared didn't understand his fathers' violent reaction. He was unable to defend himself against brutality inflicted by his father. While he wanted to shout, "I hate you," instead he ran from the room, up the stairs, and into the sanctuary of his bedroom, flinging his body upon the bed, where his tears could safely flow freely.

A knock on the front door interrupted his emotional release. Curious, Jared crept down the stairs. A wiry figure, dressed in tattered blue jeans, denim jacket, and brown wide-brimmed hat greeted him. Stringy strands of grey hair held in place with the aid of a fabric ponytail holder made Uncle George look more like a bandit than a serious musician and vocalist.

"Hey, boy, it's Uncle Gorgy-Porgy," Uncle George said as he stepped inside the room and ruffled his nephew's short black hair. He pulled Jared to his chest, crushing him in a powerful bear hug. He loved the boy with all his heart, and was secretly envious of his brother for having such a fine son.

George set his suitcase and band equipment in the corner of the living room, asking, "Your mom and dad home?"

"Nah, they're at some party or something to raise money for the hospital. They said they'd be home by seven."

With a sly wink, Uncle George said, "We have a few hours before your uptight father makes his presence known, so how about I freshen up and then we'll play some music? Would you like that?"

"Would I," squealed Jared, his excitement mounting.

"That's what I thought you'd say. We'll set up in the garage, then." At the foot of the stairs, he turned and said, "Spare bedroom's still first door on the left, right?"

"Sure is, Uncle George. Okay if I carry your equipment out to the garage so it's ready for you?"

"Well, if you think you can handle it, son, go for it."

"Great, thanks," Jared said, excitement evident in his tone.

As his uncle unpacked and settled in, Jared moved the microphone/amplifier mixer into the garage that already contained a large speaker system. All that needed to be done was hooking the system up. Though he wanted to start the process, he knew he'd be wiser to wait for Uncle George. Restless though he was, Jared sat on the barstool, thumping his fingers against the smooth marble surface of the bar top in anticipation.

Within a few minutes, Uncle George entered and went straight to the amp system. As he plugged the system into the speakers he asked, "Anything special you want to hear?"

"Hunger Among the Multitude."

"Sure thing. That one happens to be my favorite, too."

The air filled with electrifying sound. His uncle sang in a clear, enticing voice, "Hide your eyes, and hide your ears from all the misery. Children cry rivers of tears unknown to you or me. Hunger brings pain so fierce they'll eat the dirt beneath their feet. Mothers' breasts dried of milk, nothing left for their babies. Hunger among the multitudes; leaving our young destitute, why can't we set them free? It could be you or me."

The chords he strummed and the notes he picked evoked in Jared the same emotions of despondency and futility they had done to listeners long ago when the song was first released.

Jared found himself touched by the music in a way he'd never experienced and brushed away tears he could not control. He turned away, not wanting Uncle George to see his weakness.

The music ceased in one last thunderous burst of crescendo, then Jared felt rough, calloused fingers tilt his head upward.

"No reason to feel shame. Hell, Jared, you've given me validation of the piece. If it won't bring tears to the eyes, then I'm playing it wrong. Those tears are the highest compliment you could ever give me."

His uncle's words were welcome, but brought little solace. Jared felt childish for exhibiting such a flaw in the presence of the person he held in high esteem. He was sure his uncle thought him a girly-boy, regardless of the comforting words. He slanted his head down in shame and embarrassment as he wiped the remnants of tears from his blue eyes.

Uncle George said, "Wait here. I'll be right back."

Jared sat on the beige loveseat in front of the four-paned window on the side of the garage. Curious, he leaned forward, pulling the white lace curtains to one side. Parked at the curb was his uncle's classic '64 red Ferrari. Jared made a mental note to get a car just like it when he got old enough to drive. It was so cool.

With the sound of a door slamming shut, Uncle George returned to place a 1966 Fender Stratocaster Lake Placid Blue guitar on his nephew's lap. Jared ran his fingers over the shiny body. He would name it Blue.

Blue would become the young boy's solace, joy, and passion for years to come.

***

Yolanda entered the office, speech in hand, placing it before him on the finely polished mahogany desktop.

"Thank you, Yolanda." He gestured her to take a seat in the wooden chair next to his desk. "Let's take a look at it."

Jared scanned the document, confident in Yolanda's expertise.

He glanced at his Rolex, saw it was past Yolanda's quitting time. "Mind staying a bit longer so I can try this out on you?"

From experience, Yolanda knew it was coming. Jared was the definitive showman, always eager to be on-stage. She found his egotistical displays overbearing and presumptuous.

"Of course, Mr. Williams. I'm all ears."

Rising, Jared took the stance of an accomplished thespian, cleared his throat and began. "I'm happy to be here this evening to speak with our valued members of the Small Business Association of Sacramento. Without your support and investment in our community, the city of Sacramento would offer few jobs for our youth, stalled growth, and a grim future ...."

His voice droned in her ears. Blah, blah, blah, another bogus performance to convince the small business owners their high tax level was necessary and persuade them to believe the one and only Governor Williams was on their side. If only those poor shop owners knew the reason Jared Williams concerned himself with their organization was solely to remain in their favor and keep the votes coming in. He didn't give a damn about any one of them.

Yolanda concealed her disdain, remaining quiet until she was dismissed.

Chapter Two
Warm Welcome

It had been a hectic week. Angela Frank surveyed the small kitchen that opened into an expansive living room currently cluttered by an assortment of moving boxes. She was barely able to walk from one room to the other without tripping over something. She sighed, anticipating unpacking and settling into her new home in Roseville. She was apprehensive about the upheaval of her family and friends, Euclid and Karman, from the tranquil life they'd left back in Raleigh. She wondered if it had been the right thing to do, moving to this small suburb of Sacramento. But they'd discussed it and agreed that the move wasn't a choice; it was a commitment made when they had joined forces with the universe two years ago.

As Angela had told them, it wasn't the end. It was the beginning of transforming the mindset of the world. They'd made a small dent when the spiritual light had revealed itself to the townspeople of Raleigh, sparking a growing awareness of what can be accomplished when a town works toward the good of humanity.

Angela knew her greatest challenge was yet to come and prayed she'd be strong enough to see it through to completion.

The barking of their large dog Gumption alerted her to the fact her family was home.

Alexis and Alicia, twin whirlwinds of energy, blew into the kitchen. Beautiful pre-adolescents, nearing nine years old, they were inquisitive about the world in which they lived. Alicia focused more on nature and the beauty of the world, while Alexis was the curious, knowledge-seeking one.

They'd once enjoyed dressing alike to confuse their friends; it was difficult to tell them apart. Now they insisted on their own style of hair and clothing. Alexis wore her hair in a short bob and wore jeans and tennis shoes. Alicia's hair was long and loose, pulled away from her face with a barrette or headband; she wore frilly lace tops over short skirts or cropped pants.

"Mom, I'm starving to death," Alexis bellowed as she plopped herself down on the kitchen chair and propped her elbows on the table, scowling.

"Do you have anything decent to eat or am I stuck with carrot sticks and celery again?"

"Did someone say carrots?" Alicia rushed to take a seat next to her twin. "Yummy!

"Look, girls, we have tons of unpacking to do and I am not going food shopping until this kitchen is cleaned and everything's in place. Look in the bag on the counter. I think there are cookies, crackers, and popcorn that survived the ride. We'll get some take-out when your father gets here."

As the twins made their way to the counter, confused and excited Gumption skidded across the smooth tile floor, four legs flying until he rammed into Alexis's side, knocking her to the floor. Angela and Alicia laughed so hard they had to hold their aching stomachs.

"Stop it. Quit laughing at me. I could have been hurt or knocked my brains out," Alexis shouted. "Remind me not to be around you two if I'm drowning. Lotta good you'd be."

Angela and Alicia, wrapped in each other's arms, could only laugh harder in the face of Alexis' indignation. Losing their balance, they, too, fell to the floor, joining Alexis on the cold, hard ceramic tiles. Alexis joined in the laughter and the four—Gumption included—shared a moment of unplanned togetherness.

A slimmer-than-ever Monty Frank walked in to the sight of his family sitting on the floor, reeling with laughter, tears flowing from their eyes. The only one who didn't seem to find the situation hilarious was the mournful-eyed Gumption, who approached the man of the house with his tail wagging and proceeded to lick Monty's outreached hand.

"Hey, buddy, don't look so befuddled. Haven't you figured out these girls are wacko yet?"

He petted the dog's head and long luxurious red coat before hoisting Angela to her feet.

"Don't even ask," Angela whispered in Monty's ear.

A loud growl in Monty's stomach surprised Gumption so that he jumped back, standing with ears perked up and eyes curious, which caused Angela to burst out in laughter yet again. Monty shook his head, baffled over why his need for food would be so damn hilarious. "If you can control yourselves, I'm ready to get some food. I don't know about you, but I'm starving."

He'd spoken the magic words. Alicia and Alexis jumped to their feet and raced toward the front door. After she and Monty exited, Angela locked the front door. She was walking toward their silver Ford Fiesta when a clear, soft, beatific voice whispered, "I am here with you. The time is near."

Not now. I'm not ready yet.

But the long-silent voice had obviously returned. Angela made a mental note to call Karman and Euclid when they arrived in the morning. It had been three days since she'd last spoken with either of them and she wondered if they had received any signs or messages.

Chapter Three
Hank Waterman

Hank Waterman stood on the sidewalk holding the three-month-old Havanese close to his chest. He scanned the street and noticed Jennie Ford approaching from a few feet away. For an instant, he considered freeing the young pup until the young girl had passed. Instead, he grasped the squirming dog tighter to his chest.

He watched the girl's slim figure, dressed in white canvas shorts and tight blue T-shirt, pony-tailed black hair flying in the wind as she jogged toward him. Inwardly, his thoughts turned to lust. She might be just a kid but that didn't stop his body from yearning or his groin from aching with desire. Acting the respectable male adult had its difficulties, sexual desire being one of the most challenging to conceal. His weight shifted from left leg to right while he steadied his short, wide frame.

She ran by without any acknowledgement, which really didn't surprise him any. What young woman in her right mind would find a forty-year-old, jagged-faced, balding man appealing?

The pup let out a barely audible sharp bark and wriggled in Hank's powerful arms and calloused fingers, a futile attempt to free himself from confinement.

"There, there little fella," Hank cooed in an effort to soothe the animal. "You and me are going to get along just fine, you'll see."

Hank had been at his job at the City of Sacramento's Animal Care Services longer than any other employee. His main functions consisted of the picking up of stray animals, which he'd bring back to the shelter. Years before, he'd have been called the dog catcher. Now they gave it the fancy name of Animal Rescue Service Provider, although he guessed most folks wouldn't call the city euthanizing an animal after holding it for seventy-two hours equal to animal rescue. And that was only if the animal was free from injury or sickness. They killed those poor little bastards the moment he brought them in.

There weren't many people who could stomach his job, but knowing the ultimate outcome from the bulk of his rescues didn't bother him in the least. In fact, he looked forward to every opportunity to pick up a stray dog or cat. His secret joy came from the too-few times he could volunteer to perform clean-up work and scrape their splattered remains off the city streets. What he'd give for that job—'cept it didn't pay worth a damn and the hours fluctuated depending upon necessity.

A small growl filled the silence of the afternoon and the young dog bit his captor's fingers, drawing blood.

"You little son of a bitch," Hank snarled, reflexively bringing the injured digits to his mouth, sucking the wounds and clutching the dog against his side. As Hank lifted the frightened puppy, streaks of his blood smeared its once snow-white fur.

Tucking the puppy under his jacket, Hank walked toward his '97 Ford Ranger, a smirk of disdain upon his face. The sound of offbeat rhythms, clashing chords, and flat-toned melodies filled his head.

Chapter Four
Westward Bound

Karman had never dreamed she'd ever experience life as partner, mate, or wife. She couldn't believe her dear Euclid found her sexually appealing and was shocked when, as they approached Reno, he'd proposed marriage. Of course, she'd said yes. The bond they shared was far stronger than life itself, especially since that remarkable night when they'd meditated under the old elm tree in her backyard. Sometimes that seemed a dream that drifted into memory, only showing itself on the rare occasions Euclid brought the experience up. It wasn't a delusion and it wasn't over yet. She knew when Angela called her and asked her to relocate to California that something enormous was drawing close. Karman felt it in her soul—and this time it scared her. She just wished she knew why. The ominous feelings had struck as soon as she and Euclid started their journey. She sensed Euclid was experiencing the same emotions since he wasn't his usual jovial, playful self. Nothing was said, perhaps from fear that talking about it would break the magic of their tranquil life and interrupt their happiness.

Her fantasy of a large wedding, complete with white satin dress with shimmering sequins of silver speckled throughout, gave way to a quick stop at the Marriage Bureau to pick up their license, then a trip to the Shalimar Wedding Chapel, witnesses compliments of the staff. Within three hours, she'd accepted his proposal, secured a marriage license, and become a bride. Now they were on their way to the city where they would build a new life together.

The morning sun cast a ray of light upon the mountainside; mauve tinted violet rock glistened bright from the glow. Karman sat quiet within the confinement of the passenger seat of the old, worn Chevy pickup, peering out the window, taking in the glory of the coming day. She cast a glance toward Euclid, who seemed unaffected by the magnificence and beauty of the landscape. The sight of his face, so serious and intense, made her giggle. She missed his broad smile and hearty laugh.

Karman stroked the bristled right side of Euclid's face. "Euc, why so quiet this morning?"

She shifted her body toward the left, adjusted the hem of her pink and green flowered dress, and watched his face, wondering why Euclid ignored her words. He appeared lost in thought, oblivious to the outside world.

The truth was that Euclid was incapable of responding to her conversation. His mind was filled with premonitions of the days ahead, of acts designed intent with purposeful authority. The voice, so familiar, was once again director, controller, and regulator of his destiny. So clear and perfect were the visions, so difficult the implementation. He knew it would take every bit of strength, fortitude, and commitment he possessed to carry out the work set before him.

"Have no fear my friend, I shall be beside you. I will give you aid," the voice whispered softly in his ear before releasing his mind to the present.

Euclid considered telling Karman about the reappearance of the visions and voices but decided it wasn't a good time. Once they got settled, there'd be plenty of time to discuss it.

"Euc, honey, don't you think we better find a hotel and call Angela? I'm a bit weary from the ride. Besides, I can't wait to hear her reaction when she finds we're old married folk."

"Ya don't need to worry 'bout that, sweetie pie. We'll be pullin' into the town of Folsom any minute now an' I've made arrangements fer a great restin' spot. We'll git cleaned up, refreshed a bit, and give Ang a ring. Ya got her new number handy?"

"Yes, it's in the address book in my purse. I have her number and their street address in Roseville. Boy, will she be surprised."

The answering twinkle in his eye prompted her to ask, "Are you up to some sort of mischief, my husband?"

"Now, Karman, why would you even ask such a thing?" Euclid chuckled. He knew his new bride would forgive him as soon as she saw his surprise.

In just under ten minutes, Euclid pulled the car into the driveway of their new residence. He'd bought the property with funds made by the sale of his home in Raleigh. He'd decided months ago he wanted to live the rest of his life with Karman and he wanted them to start out that life together in their own home. The small two bedroom, one bath bungalow was quaint, with a half porch wrapped from the front of the home to the side entering the kitchen. White trimmed the newly painted yellow wood exterior and, to their delight, blue-green Vitex and small Eastern Redbud trees set against each side of the home. A narrow concrete path led to the front porch stairs, set against a newly manicured lush lawn. It was tiny, yet a perfect place to call home.

"Okay, my big, beautiful woman, we've arrived."

Tears formed in Karman's eyes. It was her proverbial dream come true, and so unexpected. All she could do was gasp in delight.

"Now, yer not gonna' go cryin' on me, are ya? It's time to carry ya over the threshold," Euclid teased as he opened the passenger side door and reached in to lift her large-framed body.

The Wheel's Final Turn

"Euclid Hannigan, get your hands off me this instant before you break your back," Karman ordered, shooing him away with a soft push to his chest. "We'll walk through the doorway together as man and wife, Mr. and Mrs. Euclid Hannigan." Karman decided she could say that repeatedly and never tire of hearing it, so she said it again. "Mr. and Mrs. Euclid Hannigan." Euclid knew better than to disagree with that tone of voice. He'd been married before, and for long enough to know when to keep his big trap shut and listen. Taking Karman's hand, he led her up the stairs onto the porch, then opened the door and walked through the entrance, gently pulling his new bride in after him. Together they stepped into the arch framed foyer.

Karman sighed with pleasure at the sight of the fine architecture from years past. How appealing and picturesque it was, complete with a working fireplace.

Euclid seemed as pleased with their new residence as Karman did. His noticed a few areas needing further restoration, which appealed to his artisan inclinations. A wide smile filled his face, and his thunderous laughter echoed through the room.

"Yup, think this will suit us jist fine."

Chapter Five
Wayne Marshall

The lukewarm spray of water streamed from the shower faucet. He loved the feel of the water against his pale skin.

Emerging from the shower stall, he grabbed the fluffy white towel from the bathroom door hook and carefully dried his body, unable to avoid an erection as he ran the soft material over his private parts. Turning to the mirror, he drew a wide toothed comb through his short blonde hair and patted it in place with his hands. He studied his reflection in the mirror. Staring back was a finely chiseled face free of hair, a slim sharp nose above thin lips, and light sky-blue deep-set eyes. His body was rail thin, though muscular. He was able to eat whatever he wished and never gained an ounce, unlike his partner of two years, Ozzie Langongola.

Ozzie did his best. He'd urge Wayne to accompany him on his routine of weight lifting three times per week and, the highlight of each day, the evening jogs in Burbury Park. But Wayne would have no part of it, no matter how much his partner pleaded. Even the thought of facing others terrified him. He preferred the sanctity and safe haven of their home. Wayne hadn't left the front yard for over six months. He'd tried, truly tried, slowly placing one foot onto the concrete sidewalk, while tremors of fear took over his body and sweat dripped from each pore. Gasping for breath, he felt the world closing in on him.

It hadn't always been that way. Although each time he left his home, he'd felt a bit apprehensive, he hadn't let it stop him from enjoying life. He hadn't cared what others thought of him or his lifestyle—until a year earlier when three youthful white supremacists dragged him away from his car as he was getting in, pushing and pulling and shoving him into the dark alley between his favorite pub, Sonny's, and the One Hour Photo Shop.

He heard one of them say, "What's wrong, sissy boy, no big brute to save your ass?" Swift punches to his face, stomach, and groin followed, and he crumbled to his knees on the cold, jagged pavement. The whole while, words of hate were spit out in sneering, accusing voices. "Fucking fag." "Pansy ass." "Prick face."

A shaved-headed, muscular young man pulled him to his feet, raised his body off the ground, looked into his wide-eyed, terrified face, and laughed the cackle of a psychopathic maniac. "You worthless piece of shit, you scum-sucking dirtbag. Me and the boys are aiming to crush your sorry-assed life and send you back to hell where you belong."

Again they were on him, and he was unable to defend himself as his three attackers kicked, beat, and hurled his body against brick walls, repeatedly knocking his head into the hard surface. The last thing he remembered before he lost consciousness was feeling a large heavy object crash into his skull and the warmth of his own oozing blood as it flowed into his eyes and down his face.

Wayne cringed as he recalled the brutality and then the shame he'd felt afterwards as his name and picture was broadcasted in the media. For weeks, it seemed there wasn't a newspaper or news broadcast that didn't contain an update. He'd even made the national news. And, while they'd caught the bastards who took away the hearing in his right ear and left him with a noticeable limp, he was the one who paid the ultimate price. No longer could he venture from his home and walk freely among the people of his town without imagining their overtures as being meant to insult and humiliate.

His last excursion into the world had cemented his agoraphobia.

He'd encountered a large-busted, thin, middle-aged woman wearing a purple exercise suit in the establishment's parking lot.

"Good evening," he spoke in an upbeat, friendly voice.

The older woman eyed him from head to toe, sneered, turned her chin skyward as she glanced away, responding with a curt "Humph."

Then the checkout clerk slammed his bread and eggs into the grocery bag while the elderly man behind him muttered under his breath, "Now I have to share a line with some faggot. What's this world coming to," and shoved his cart into Wayne's right ass cheek.

He'd grabbed his grocery bag, smashed eggs and all, and run to his car. His hands quivered. His face was red with anger, his body rigid with fear as he fumbled to retrieve the keys from his pants pocket.

From that day forward, his sanctuary became his prison.

Chapter Six
New Beginnings

"Expect the doctor to arrive at eleven o'clock tomorrow morning, Mr. Marshall," Karman confirmed to the patient on the other end of the phone. "No, it's not unusual for her to make house calls in circumstances such as yours. Just be up and ready when she gets there." After a short pause, "Thank you, too, Mr. Marshall. Don't worry, you'll do fine."

Angela stuck her head through the doorway of her new office. "What have you set up for me now, Karman?"

"The man hasn't left his home in ages, so you'll be making a visit to Sacramento tomorrow morning."

Interested, Angela entered the room fully. "Agoraphobia, hmm, haven't had a case of that in a while. Of course, with my practice so new, I need all the clients I can get. Thank goodness for the referrals Dr. Striver gave me. Without those and the Kaiser Permanente Hospital's overflow, I'd have a hard time meeting our overhead. By the way, where's that new husband of yours? Wasn't he supposed to fix the running toilet in the patients' bathroom? I can hear the noise from here and it's driving me batty."

"He'll be along, don't worry. Euclid might be a bit slow in the delivery but he's a master handyman. Besides," Karman joked, "where else are you going to find someone to fix this place up for free?"

"Point well taken," Angela responded. "When's the next patient due?"

"Two o'clock. That leaves us an hour and a half to catch a bite to eat. I've been dying to try that French Restaurant, Crush 29, over on Eureka Road. Hear they have a great luncheon menu."

"You go ahead, Karman. It'll give me time to look over some charts and answer a few phone messages."

"Your call, Ang, but you'll be missing out on some excellent chow. Maybe I'll have Euclid meet me there and then bring him back to the office with me."

"Good idea. Take some extra time, married lady," Angela teased before returning to her office.

***

It had been a trying time, Angela reflected, moving into a new home, setting up the office, and trying to get the house in order so that Monty could finally work from an office there. He now coached others on how to repair their credit, providing them the information and tools needed at a minimal cost. At times, he would donate his knowledge freely when he found a creditor or financial institution had taken gross advantage of a family. The change in him was remarkable. He found true gratification in assisting others. Since he charged such minimal fees, he planned to supplement his income by holding instructive seminars throughout California. His first large seminar at the Convention Hall in Santa Clara a week earlier had brought in a pack-the-house crowd, and he had several seminars over the next four months.

Angela touched her forefinger to her forehead, looked around her office and said, "Very nice. Very nice indeed." She was proud of the job she, Euclid, and Karman had done in the renovation and décor. What were once bland, dirty, off-white walls were now painted a clear, crisp, pale, green. A '50s-style cherry wood executive desk set next to the large white-draped window. There was, of course, the compulsory overstuffed beige couch to one side. Two matching cherry wood armchairs faced the desk. All she needed to do now was hang her diplomas, licenses, and pictures and the room would be complete.

Speak to Euclid, Angela. It's up to you. He has much to do.

The voice had returned, sounding in her mind with a growing rate of recurrence over the last few days. To ignore it would only intensify it until it held her full attention. As she approached the sofa, a vision flashed across her mind's eye. She stumbled, reeled forward, catching herself by clutching onto the couch's arm and plopping onto the soft cushions.

She didn't want to think of the darkness right now. She felt ill-prepared to confront such evil.

Gentle music filled her mind, soothing her doubts with each pure tone of note.

Remember why you've come here, Angela. The time is fast approaching and I am here to protect you.

Picking up her cell phone, Angela pressed a speed dial key. On the third ring, she heard the familiar gruff voice.

"Euclid, its Ang. Got a minute?"

Chapter Seven
Alana's Plan

Misty was rushed out of the office by two uniformed security guards who guided her to her work cubicle. Her face was red with shame, embarrassment, and humiliation. She stifled the tears waiting to flow freely from her downcast eyes. She was going to leave with dignity. Her co-workers were shocked to see one of their favorite people under what was tantamount to armed guard. Misty doing something adverse to the best interest of the company was not something anyone had ever thought possible.

For herself, Misty didn't understand why her supervisor, Mr. Reynolds, would accuse her of such impropriety. She replayed the scene in her head, trying to make sense of it.

Her day had begun like any other. A thirty-minute workout on the treadmill, a quick shower, bowl of oatmeal with fresh berries, hair and makeup, dressed in a soft cashmere sweater over skinny jeans and off to the train station, destination San Francisco's Market Street, the headquarters of C & M Enterprises.

She was the spokeswoman for the Youthful Renewal line of cosmetics, with a staff of ten who worked together diligently to promote the product. Morgan Lavonovich had transformed herself into gorgeous Misty Lane, known the world over for her simple, elegant beauty confessed as the result of diligently using the Youthful Renewal creams, serums, and makeup. She stood a full five feet eleven inches tall, had warm beige skin, round hazel eyes, full pouty lips, and thick long brown hair. Weighing only one hundred and twenty pounds was a plus when fitting into those skin tight jeans or close fitted designer dresses the manufacturers paid her to wear at fashion events.

She'd arrived at work, admittedly a few minutes late, to find her assistant standing at her office doorway, a look of sadness and apprehension on her chubby face.

"Reynolds called and said he needed to see you as soon as you got her. He's waiting in his office."

Misty nodded, turned, and trekked down the long hallway leading to Reynolds' office, where she found her boss looking out the picture window that took up most of the wall. He motioned her to sit on the chair nearest his desk. The look on his evenly tanned face troubled her. He seemed ill at ease, his normally carefree attitude replaced by a sternness she had never encountered during their four years together.

"Look, Misty, I'm going to make this short. No use beating around the bush. Avante Grande released their latest cosmetic line yesterday, Young Love, Long Love. They claim to have a secret ingredient that allows their stuff to go from solid to liquid and be absorbed into the skin immediately. It also covers birthmarks, red marks, blemishes, and provides a smooth even surfacing of the skin wherever applied. Get this, Ms. Lane. Not only does it cover all pores, it refinishes the skin to an airbrushed texture".

He approached her and peered into her startled eyes. "Any of this sound familiar to you? Ring a bell or two?"

"I don't understand. If you're asking if I realize we're due to release the latest Youthful Renewal line that provides essentially the same results, then, yes, that rings true. But if you're implying I knew anything about this, you're wrong. I would never compromise my career or this company by doing anything so underhanded. How in the world did this happen?

Her boss looked at her as if she was a mortal enemy.

"You cannot possibly think I would leak our secrets to Avante Grande."

"How else, then, Misty? You and I were the only two people alive who knew the complete formula and that we were to announce it this coming Friday."

"Well, the chemists had to know what's in it. There's tons of people, including the laboratory assistants, who could gain access to the formulas. For God's sake, John, there are a lot of people who would benefit from doing this."

"Maybe so, but only one person acted and sold us out. That person, my dear, would be you."

"Why would I do such a thing? C & M Industries has been my entire life. I'd be an idiot to throw it away, especially at this stage in my career."

"Misty, you must think I'm a fool. I know Avante Grande has asked you to join their operation." He grabbed a piece of paper from his desk and thrust it toward her. "What's your explanation for this, then? Is this a signed contact or not?"

She took it from him and began to read. "Where did you get this garbage? You think I'm jumping ship? Is that it?"

"Isn't that your signature, Ms. Lane? I'd know it anywhere."

"I swear, John, that is *not* my signature. I've never seen this before."

He stood, grabbed the phone, pushed two buttons, and in a measured monotone said, "Get security in here." He looked at Misty and, face filled with hatred, pounded his left hand onto the desk with such force that paperweights, pens, and papers flew onto the beige carpeted floor.

"There's no fast talking your way out of this one, Ms. Lane. You know, we took you from nothing and made you into a superstar. This is how you show your gratitude? I'm not listening to any more of your lies, you ungrateful little bitch. Get out of my sight."

Before Misty could react, two armed security guards entered the room, each taking one of her arms, and led her out of the office. She'd just been fired from the job of her dreams, her hard work and dedication meaningless, over something she knew nothing about and had not been involved in. Anger and frustration gave way to tears as she was watched carefully while she collected her personal belongings.

***

Alana emerged from behind the dense dark brown curtains; it was safe to come out of her hiding place now that Reynolds was off to an appointment. Adrenalin surged through her lithe body. It had been risky, sneaking in and concealing her presence, but she wouldn't have missed it for anything. She snickered, satisfied her work was done. Now she would shine. It would be up to her to lead the new Youthful Renewal line into full glory. Those hours of studying and practicing arrogant, prissy Misty Lane's signature had proven worth the effort.

Lifting the edges of her A-line skirt, she spun around and pranced in front of the full-length mirror attached to the office wall. She kicked up her heels and drew closer to the mirror, examining her youthful face. The reflection staring back was a perfect oval face framing eyes best described as cat-like. Her eyes could hold pure innocence, intense sexuality, but, most appealing, deep mystery. No one looked into Alana Colbert's eyes without stopping a moment to gaze deeper, as though mesmerized, captivated. Her attitude of friendliness and look of innocence captured people's hearts.

But what was reflected in the mirror was a facade. For her, the rail-thin, long-legged dancer's body, ample bosom, and lush, sparkling natural blonde hair cascading down her back were merely the means to an end, granting her preference over the less attractive, but, most of all, giving her a true sense of superiority.

A smug smile on her gorgeous face, ignoring the discordant music that played in the recesses of her mind, Alan decided she'd have to thank the strange old man who'd approached her with the unsigned contract in hand. It had worked to perfection.

Chapter Eight
Relaxation

His thick fingers fumbled at the output jack. He recognized the importance of being precise so that the change to the guitar would be unnoticeable. With deed completed, he silently placed the instrument back into the rear of the closet, closed the door, and made a swift exit through the open window.

***

Jared sat on the edge of his bed, clad in only beige boxer shorts and white socks, holding his dear guitar Blue to his chest. He'd like nothing more than to walk away from politics and spend the rest of his life playing his music. No amount of sex, money, or prestige held more meaning than the pleasure he got playing music.

The surface of his guitar glistened, throwing off reflections of purple and lavender light. Jared picked each string, adjusting it until the instrument was in perfect pitch. He'd bought other guitars but none produced the tone and richness of his Blue. He stood, plugged in the amp, turned up the volume, and strummed the first chord. An electric shock filled his entire body as an invisible force threw him across the room. His left shoulder hit the jutting edge of the armoire before his body crashed to the floor. Jared clutched himself against the pain; drool fell from his mouth onto the expensive Persian rug, mingling with the gold and blue threads before sinking into the plush fabric and vanishing. He shook his head, trying to clear it. Blue lay against the end table, shining bright, as if mocking him to return and play a few random chords.

Trembling, Jared gripped the edge of the armoire and cautiously rose to his feet. He'd have to take Blue and the amp and get them repaired.

***

Euclid rose from the bushes surrounding the governor's bedroom and dusted off his worn blue jeans and khaki jacket. Ang was right. It had begun.

Chapter Nine
Home Again

Angela lay on the overstuffed mint-green sofa and snuggled under the thin blue-and-rose plaid throw, finally able to relax now that the twins were fast asleep. Monty was out of town at another speaking engagement. She was proud of how he'd changed the course of his life in such a positive way. She stretched her arms, adjusted the throw pillow behind her, and lay back with her head resting on the sofa's cushiony arm.

The stillness of the night was welcome after a hectic day of patients, traffic jams, and grocery shopping. She picked up the remote from the pocket attached to the couch and turned on the television. On the 50 inch screen was yet another commentator broadcasting the day's most depressing news. Angela quickly switched channels; she was tired of the mindless drone of the media. She hoped to find a show that would either make her laugh or teach her something, but the airwaves seemed filled with nothing but mindless drivel: an ad for the latest iPad, a woman selling butt-enhancing lingerie, a murder for hire crime show, young women throwing punches, a credit card commercial. She switched the television off. *And we pay good money for this?*

Gumption rose from the floor to nuzzle her hand.

"Aw, Gumption', I love you, too, you big, clumsy goof." She grasped the side of the dog's head with both hands, looked into his mournful eyes, and planted a kiss on his wet nose. In return, Gumption landed several sloppy, wet licks on her nose and checks, his tail wagging happily at the attention.

"All right, that's enough." Angela laughed, pushing him away and wiping her face. She wondered if it was too late to call Euclid and Karman to see when they could get together. She couldn't put it off much longer; it was clear that they must reach the source once more. Like it or not, they had been given a huge responsibility that could not be ignored or cast aside.

"Go ahead. They are waiting for your call," rang in her ears.

This time she'd speak with Karman. Euclid would never refuse his wife. She lifted the wireless phone from its holder and dialed.

***

His stomach full from the baked lemon chicken, brown buttered rice and slivered almond string beans, Euclid produced a loud, extended burp. He patted his protruding belly, pulled his sinking jeans up, and started toward the porch. The rich walnut rocker he'd crafted sat next to the white wicker swing amidst pansy filled clay pots hanging from the small porch's rafters.

After settling comfortably into the rocker, Euclid pulled his weathered carving knife from his left jean pocket and a bit of basswood from the right. Automatically, he began the process of shaving pieces from the wood's surface. Whittling was fast becoming a lost art. He guessed people thought of it as some hillbilly hobby, or maybe thought it was too difficult. But for him, the activity brought calm and pleasure. He imagined he'd be a whittler until the day his fingers could no longer hold a piece of wood or handle the sharpness of the knife. At Karman's urging, he'd set up a booth to sell his carved beauties at the local flea market. Much to his surprise, the patrons loved his work, purchasing the key chains, puzzles, caricatures, boxes, planters, and jewelry he'd taken such pleasure in crating. He felt pride in his art. And word of his creations spread. He found the demand growing. He'd wondered how he would do his share to contribute to household finances, but suddenly he was earning much more than he'd ever dreamed possible, and from doing the work he loved most.

He listened to the swallows, sparrows, and finches chirping in the distance while a soft breeze sent a tingle across his nose and chin, fingers and blade working in unison as he chipped away. In the kitchen, Karman hummed a sweet tune as she washed the dinner dishes. It filled his heart with joy to once again hear the sounds of a woman in his home. The familiar sounds of the kitchen faucet and clang of the dishes placed in the dishwasher brought back feelings long forgotten, emotions he'd shared in his former marriage with his beloved Gina before cancer had taken her away. A few years ago, he'd never imagined he'd be this content again. It felt good.

The ring of the phone interrupted his reverie. After a brief exchange, Karman came out and handed the phone to him. "It's Angela."

The hairs on the back of his neck stood up. He'd expected this call but still felt hesitant about taking it. Placing the cell to his ear, he glanced at Karman, locking eyes full of apprehension. "Howdy, Ang. What's cookin'?"

Chapter Ten
In the Presence of Hank

He squealed in pain as his small body hit the side of the cold steel cage. His stomach ached with hunger, and his body shook in fear. This was a far cry from the loving care of his owners. The young pup didn't know how to react to the treatment other than to take a firm stance and growl from deep within his throat.

A cold splash of water soaked his soft white fur, plastering it to his body. He shivered and trembled as he shook it off.

Hank staggered as he backed away from the cage, a bottle of Jim Bean in hand. He snorted, took a large swig of the burning liquor, and rubbed his hand across his mouth.

"Shut up before you get more of the same. And I don't think your lame growling is going to save your sorry ass."

The dog backed away from the harsh voice, seeking an escape but finding none as he once more crashed into the hard steel of the cage.

Hank approached again, crouched down on one knee and tossed a bit of leftover chicken into the cage. The pup, not sure the gesture could be trusted, stealthily crept toward the chicken, sniffed it, and looked up at Hank for reassurance. Sensing no danger, he devoured the meat in seconds. Wanting more, he ran toward Hank, hitting the metal rails full force, propelling him backward. He whimpered in pain and surprise.

"Ha-ha, you stupid animal. So you think you're getting more, do you? I wouldn't hold my breath if I was you, fella."

Hank pulled a Pall Mall filter from his shirt pocket, lit it, inhaled, crouched down in front of the cage, reached his hand in and touched the pup's forehead with the burning cherry. A knock at the door startled him and he pulled back before the burning ember seared the dog's skin.

"I'll get back to you later."

He rose, dropped the cigarette on the concrete floor, and crushed it with his boot before making the climb up the stairs and through the basement doorway. After adjusting his shirt collar, Hank approached and opened the front door.

A small box wrapped in plain brown paper stood at his feet. Hank looked to his right then to his left to see who might have delivered the package. With the exception of three young boys playing basketball next door and a few cars passing by, the street and yards were empty. He picked up the package, closed and locked the door, and carried the box into the kitchen where he sat at the corner table. No address, return or mailing, showed on the unadorned paper. Hank carefully examined all sides of the neatly wrapped box and held it to his ear. Hearing nothing, he shook it, making the contents rattle.

What the hell? He ripped apart the wrapping to discover a plain white box, the sort found at any department store or post office. Lifting the top of the box, he was surprised to find a man's leather belt and bracelet inside. When he picked them up a small piece of paper dropped to the tabletop. Hank snatched it up and began reading the scribbled, though legible, writing. He scratched his head and read it aloud, "It's time to change the path you lead. For justice lies in wait for those who harm the innocent and the unarmed. Beware! These words are yours to heed."

"What the hell?" This time he spoke the thought aloud.

It never occurred to him that anyone could have discovered his cruel nature. He was much too careful for that.

Dismissing the note as some sick prank meant for someone else and mistakenly delivered to his door, he turned his attention to the belt and bracelet in his hand. He could feel their softness as he inhaled the fresh aroma only new leather emits. Hank strung the belt through the loops on his jeans, being sure to buckle it tight, then clamped the leather bracelet on his right wrist. He was certain the package wasn't meant for him, but just as certain he would keep the gifts as his own. He spared one fleeting thought for the jerk who was intended to receive such fine gifts. To be the recipient of such a prophetic note, he must have really pissed somebody off.

As Hank slugged down more rum, the warm gold tone of the finely whittled eagle belt buckle and the bracelet's inlayed owl carvings glowed softly.

Chapter Eleven
Stepping Up

Wayne didn't care if he ever saw the outside world again. If not for his deep love for Ozzie, he would never have made the appointment with the psychiatrist. He enjoyed spending his days preparing fine cuisine, maintaining the impeccable order of their home, and indulging in his greatest love of all, oil painting. His landscapes of the Sacramento area had caught the eye of William Rogers of the famed Rogers Art Gallery. Rogers had an eye for sellable art and set up a showing, selecting a diverse range of paintings from Wayne's abundant reserve. People fell in love with his soft brushstrokes and infinite detail of color, and soon he'd been able to live off the commissions made from his sales. Rogers was willing to arrange transport of his paintings to the gallery — as long as it was profitable.

Wayne painted under the name of Eli Sanborne. The pseudonym gave him the ability to be inconspicuous while receiving the notoriety he had earned. The fact no one had ever seen the mysterious Eli Sanborne only added to the appeal. There were several internet sites offering a grand prize to anyone who could find the elusive artist. For the time being, his agoraphobia and a particular clause in his contract with the gallery provided complete obscurity.

He knew that it bothered Ozzie that he, Wayne, was unable to join him in his outside activities. Ozzie's oft-stated fondest desire was to have an intimate dinner at The Firehouse, catch a show, and finish the evening off at Badland's Bar, sipping champagne and reveling in their love. Finally giving in to his partner's request that he seek help, Wayne had reluctantly promised Ozzie he'd try the shrink business and had just as reluctantly set up an appointment with Dr. Angela Frank.

He glanced at the cuckoo clock as the small bird exited, chirping the hour in its sharp, distinct whistle of cuc-koo, cuc-koo, ten times. He jumped at the sound of the doorknocker rap, rap, rapping. No getting out of it now. The doctor had arrived, right on schedule.

Wayne slowly approached the front door and looked through the eyehole to see a very attractive, slim blonde woman dressed in a navy-skirted suit, holding a large briefcase. He wondered if he'd made a mistake. She didn't look old enough to be a head-shrinker. He considered ignoring her and searching for an older, more experienced professional. As an added bonus, her apparent lack of age and, by association, experience in the field would be a great excuse to give Ozzie. *What the hell*, he reasoned as he opened the door, *she's here. Might as well let her in.*

"Mr. Marshall?" The woman said, holding out her hand.

Wayne nodded, and returned her firm squeeze.

"Please come in, Doctor. I've been expecting you." After an uneasy moment of silence, Wayne asked, "I'm new to this. Do we do the old couch routine? The family room is through the kitchen."

"Mr. Marshall—"

"Please call me Wayne."

"Fine, Wayne. Why don't we sit at a table? The couch, though necessary at times, is somewhat of a myth. Most of the time, my patients sit in a comfortable chair."

Wayne clasped his hands. "I see. Well, then, I think my partner's office will be the perfect place." He motioned Angela to follow him.

Angela had to agree that the room was ideal. Two sky-blue microfiber upholstered chairs sat in the center around a square glass-topped table. A large light oak desk ran the length of the far wall. White lace curtains covered the picture window to the desk's left side, with mallard green- and navy blue-striped drapes framing either end.

"Mr. Marshall— I mean Wayne, please sit. And by all means relax. You look terrified. Believe me, I don't bite."

Angela slid into the opposite chair, placing her briefcase to one side.

"Today I'm going to concentrate on background information. We'll get into other areas of therapy once I have a clearer picture of how extensive your phobia is. There are many things that might help, but each person's unique, so today we'll just be talking."

Wayne relaxed as he sank into the overstuffed chair. The fear and anxiety drained from his face. *Maybe this shrink knows her stuff after all.*

Angela proceeded to get information on his family, education, health, and lifestyle. When Wayne talked about facing the outside world, he described it as if a dark, terrifying force was holding him back. When he told her about the brutal beating and humiliation of having his name splashed across the country's media, Angela's heart broke.

Without knowing how she knew, Angela knew Wayne Marshall had a large part to play in the upcoming battle. She was determined to help him.

Part II

INTERVENTION

Comes a time in life to face reality
of acts and deeds once done,
to show humility.
Yet can one be this brave,
to look so deep inside?
Under the façade,
reveal your inner grave?
Accept the hand that offers help,
or continue as before?
A fleeting glance of destiny
shakes you to the core.

~Monica Brinkman, 2014

Chapter 12
Winning at the Game

As Alana expected, she was offered the position of spokesperson for the Youthful Renewal line of cosmetics. That she'd been screwing the pants off old man Lucas, who'd headed the board since the company began, didn't hurt. "Men are so easy to manipulate," thought Alana, chuckling over her triumph. It hadn't been easy caressing and kissing his wrinkled, shriveled body. She had to stifle her gag response every time she gave the old geezer a blow job. Thank God he couldn't manage an erection for more than a second. The thought of his teeny-weeny peeny revolted her, but, had it come to actual sex, she'd have given the performance of her lifetime, aided by her secret ally, the music. It egged her on, instilled pure power, methodically prodded her with a melody sinister and dark. It had become her weapon of choice, always there when she evoked it.

Alana stretched out her arms, tilted back in her ergonomic office chair, and surveyed her new surroundings. The office, though tiny, was all hers. Smugness turned to professionalism as John Reynolds voice came through the speakerphone.

"Alana, pick up."

Snatching the receiver, she purred, "I'm all ears, John. What's up?"

She listened, placed the receiver back in its spot, then pushed back her chair and stood to smooth her skirt and fluff her curls before answering his summons.

Reynolds opened the door in response to her perfunctory knock and motioned her to the chair in front of his desk. He peered out into the hall before shutting the door securely and returning to his seat. John stared directly into Alana's eyes, scrutinizing her reaction. Pleased when she returned the stare without hesitation or turning from his glance, he said, "Can't be too cautious with what's recently happened."

Alana nodded her agreement.

"I assume you received the contract from Legal and have read the confidentiality conditions?"

"Yes, sir, I read them, signed the contract, and returned it to Brewer's secretary this morning."

"Good."

Reynolds stood, turning his back to Alana for a moment, rubbing the nape of his neck before turning back to her, fire in his eyes. "I'm saying this only once, and you better heed my words if you want a future with this company." The volume of his voice rose slightly as emphasis to his next words. "I will not tolerate unethical business practices for your personal gain. Hear me clearly, if I have an inkling of doubt about your loyalty to this organization, I will ruin not only your career here but also your reputation in the industry. Do you understand?"

Without hesitation came the answer, "Yes, Mr. Reynolds. I understand completely. I promise you, I'll never give you a reason to doubt my allegiance to this company. I worked my ass off as Misty Lane's publicity agent and am as horrified as you that she sold us out"

"Good to hear, Alana. I don't doubt you; I just wanted to set the record straight before we go forward with the campaign and our working relationship."

Alana smiled and extended her hand. John clasped it in a firm handshake, sealing their partnership, satisfied they'd selected the perfect woman to represent Youthful Renewal.

***

His rough hands groped for the small bottle of Youthful Renewal shampoo. Ever so carefully he turned the cap and placed it on top of the bathroom sink. A few drops would do the trick. Guided by *Careful, not too much. Yes, that's perfect,* he replaced and tightened the cap, then set the bottle back in the bathroom cabinet.

Chapter Thirteen
Spoken Like a True Politician

Jared pulled the thick velour curtains aside enough to eye the flow of people entering the auditorium. "Quite a crowd," he thought, understanding most were independent business owners. He'd had no idea there'd be such a large turnout. It was either an ominous sign of unrest or one of great support. How these meetings would turn out was unpredictable, and that terrified him. After all his years in the public eye, speaking engagements continued to unnerve him. Drops of sweat formed on his face, quickly wiped away with an exquisitely embroidered handkerchief. Jared felt the pressure of a hand on his left forearm and turned to see a young, skinny, pimple-faced security guard who nodded to let Jared know it was almost time.

As he entered the stage and sat in his assigned seat to the right of the podium with the young security guard seated beside and slightly behind him, he heard the crowd rustle. Bright lights blinded his view of individuals; all he was able to make out were forms rushing to seats. The lights dimmed, silently announcing that the event would soon start, as Chief Police Arnold Angst took his place before the platform. Lights up, and it was time for the show.

A bearded, middle-aged man sat in the rear corner of the auditorium, eyes staring straight ahead as he shifted his weight from one side to the other. He removed his cotton khaki hat and placed it on the vacant seat to his left, a smile of contentment on his tightly closed lips. Chief Angst droned on endlessly, his attempts at humor bringing only silence. The man was embarrassed for the official, and wished he'd conclude his remarks.

As if on cue, Chief Angst said, "Ladies and gentlemen of the Small Business Association, I'm sure you've waited in anticipation to hear from none other than the governor of this fine state of California. So without further ado, I present to you Governor Jared Williams."

A round of applause filled the room as Jared took his place behind the wooden podium.

His hands trembled as he positioned his pre-written speech, cleared his throat, and exhaled. He smiled broadly; brilliant lights glistened off perfect white teeth.

"Thank you, Chief Angst, for that wonderful introduction. It's not only an honor, it's a privilege to speak before you this evening." Feedback screeched, cutting off his words. People held their hands to their ears as the harsh tones vibrated from front to back, side to side, ceiling to floor. Whimpers of pain swept through the crowd. Within seconds, there was complete silence.

Jared adjusted his shirt collar, moved closer to the podium, and, with hesitation, spoke softly into the microphone, not certain of the outcome.

"Please forgive the technical difficulties." Hearing that his voice was clear, he continued, "The governor's job is to seek growth for the state. Growth of agriculture, increase of available wares, affordable pricing, and, ultimately, a rise in new business ventures. So how does a state facing budget restrictions make that happen? Simple. We encourage small business with an incentive. An incentive called tax exemptions, such as the newly founded Hire and Teach program. So far, we've saved small business thousands of dollars while at the same time providing hands-on training to our youth. We must consider our future and the future of the next generations as they take on the challenges of those who have gone before them. I call this a win/win situation. How about you? Are you with me?"

The crowd broke into thunderous applause. At the sound of their enthusiasm, Jared grasped the microphone with both hands. His eyes bulged, his tongue protruded from his gaping mouth as violent spasms shook his body. The last thing he was aware of before he lost consciousness was a warm stream running down his pants leg.

***

The bearded man placed his cotton khaki hat back on his head and exited the auditorium. Two paramedics whisked past him, one brushing the arm of his jacket.

He whistled as he walked toward the safety of his car. The wheel had been set in motion. The time was drawing near.

Chapter Fourteen
A Woman Always Knows

Karman knew something had been weighing heavy on Euclid's mind for a few days. She'd hoped he would share his troubles with her openly without the need for her to ask. The last thing she wanted to be was a nagging wife. And she had to admit that it hurt a little that he didn't turn to her. So, even though she hated to, she decided she had to confront him.

The oven timer buzzed, interrupting her thoughts. She scurried to the stove and opened the oven door to a scrumptious-looking homemade apple pie. The smell of cinnamon, sugar, and apples permeated the room as she pulled dessert out and placed it upon the countertop.

"Sweetie, I'm home", came the gruff male voice she had grown to love. He entered the kitchen and gave her a bear hug from behind.

"Now, stop that. Can't you see I'm baking", she teased, loosening his fingers from around her thick waist and turning to give him a quick peck on the cheek.

"Come here, woman," he growled, drawing Karman close to his broad chest. "Those chores can wait. Besides, never a time too busy to give my Missus some lovin'."

Karman pulled away, and taking his hand in hers, led him to the kitchen table.

"Euclid, we have to talk."

Solemn, Euclid replied, "Of course. Is something wrong?"

"Perhaps you should be answering that particular question, Euclid. You've been in such deep thought lately that you don't even hear me when I speak to you. Now, what on earth is on your mind? Is it the phone call from Angela?"

Euclid looked away for a second, collecting his thoughts. He should have known Karman would notice his preoccupation. And he had no real reason for not telling her about the sweet music and encouraging voices that were increasing with each passing day—other than to spare her a little time before the final commitment.

In an uncharacteristically low, soft voice he said, "It's happening to me again, Karman. The voices, the music, frequent and persistent. I've complied as best I can to perform this service of care for humanity. I fear the time draws near fer us to face the evil that preys upon this world."

Euclid paused and examined his wife's reaction, pleased to see she was nodding in understanding. He rose from the chair, his voice rising as he turned his face to the ceiling, the nothingness, and bellowed, "Dear

God, ye must see I'm a simple man without great courage or wisdom. I don't know why ye picked me fer this mission and maybe ole Euclid will never understand yer reasoning, but, please, I beg you, don't let harm come to my wonderful wife. I jist couldn't take it."

Tears filled Karman's eyes as she rushed to his side to hold him close, to offer comfort. To ease his mind, she said, "You old fool. Can't you see I'm just as much a part of this journey as you? You don't ever have to hide what's in your heart. I'm here to share this duty, to give you confidence, inspiration, and, if necessary, guidance."

Karman held Euclid's face in her hands and kissed him before saying, "We'll get through this together, Euclid. As long as we have each other, we're a powerful force to reckon with. No one and nothing can come between us. But I need you to promise one thing to me now, that you will always turn to me in times of worry."

Euclid nodded, a bit ashamed he had chosen not to in the first place.

Angelic harmony filled Karman's ears, perfect in pitch, joyous in melody, calming her soul. More, it gave her the strength of conviction.

Chapter Fifteen
Reflection

Monty plopped his legs onto the round tufted ottoman and leaned his head on Angela's shoulder, enjoying the bond they had formed over the last two years. He snuggled closer, thinking how great it was to be home. His job brought satisfaction, but took him away from his treasured family. But the fact he was helping the desperate who were on the verge of losing their homes, their investments, their savings, far outweighed his personal desires.

So much had changed since *that day* in Raleigh. The experience had altered his entire outlook on life, as well as his attention to his health. The once overweight, sluggish young father had trimmed to a perfect weight of one hundred seventy pounds and his energy level zoomed. Now he could experience each moment of his life to the fullest. No longer did he feel the need to hide from the outside world behind a computer. He could meet people face-to-face and share his knowledge. He had been given a second chance.

"Daddy, come here."

Monty exchanged a knowing glance with Angela before rising and making his way up the stairs to his twin daughters' room. Alexis was attempting to secure a row of long, dangling bronze and silver beads to the top of the closet frame using two-sided tape. The door, once held in place by hinges was laying atop her bed. *What on earth is she doing now?*

"What's up, Alex?"

"I can't reach the top, Daddy,"

Muffling a laugh, he offered," Tell you what, kiddo, why don't I put some hooks on the top and you can loop those beads around them."

"Could you?" she squealed with delight. "That would be excellent."

"You were planning to sleep on the door?"

"Oh, Daddy, of course not. That would be silly."

"Guess I could make some room in the garage for it. Tell you what, I'll take the door down and bring back the hooks." Monty grabbed the door and carefully maneuvered it through the bedrooms doorway. "Be back in a jiff."

Alexis couldn't wait to surprise Alicia and hoped she'd have the beads hung by the time her sister got home from the library. Monty returned, hooks in hand, and began screwing them into the top of the doorframe. Carefully, he draped the metal eye over the newly placed hooks. Within ten minutes, his handiwork was completed, and each long string of beads sparkled in the rays of light flowing through the bedroom window. Alexis smiled with pride and Monty was content.

They heard the downstairs door open and shared a knowing look as Alicia bounded up the stairs and her footsteps grew near. She rushed into the bedroom, threw her books on her bed, and turned to look at her father and sister. "What? Why are you two looking at me that way?" Before they could answer, Gumption raced into the room and made a beeline to the closet, beads clanking and swaying as he entered. The startled dog cowered in fear, looking up at his humans, strands of beads falling on his face, his snout stuck out between them. Monty and the twins laughed and Alicia ran to Gumption, pulling him out of the closet. "Bad dog," she scolded and led Gumption out of the bedroom before closing the door.

"Well, girls, I think old Gumption proved the strands will hold. Don't know about you two, but I could go for an ice cream. Any takers?"

Without hesitation, the girls raced down the stairs to the kitchen. Monty followed slowly. He all of a sudden felt uneasy. In the corner of his mind whispered a familiar melody. The hair on the back of his neck stood up. He'd thought this was in the past. Was the evil back?

"Are you going to have ice cream or not?" Alexis called.

***

Sotto voce, the words entered her mind. *Go to him. He is in need of your strength. Do not waver.* Monty's face flashed before her. She could hear his laughter coming from the kitchen. Angela joined her family. Monty turned toward her and their eyes locked.

She was not prepared emotionally or intellectually to begin the fight. At least not yet.

Yes, you are. And it is nearer than you know.

Angela held an empty bowl out. "What the hell, make mine two scoops."

Chapter Sixteen
Waterman's Welcome

He struggled to avoid looking at the rumbling black mass enticing him to enter the throbbing doorway, the beat beckoning him forward. The low, off-pitch, grumbling notes grew louder, shrieking and clashing a musical dance of madness. The power of its call was so great he had to avert his eyes from the mounting volume, the mass growing larger and larger until it embraced him with its intensity, filling all space, leaving him no room for escape.

The once sunlit room was encased in the blackest of darkness, filled with the pulsing beat of iniquity. Hank, once fearful, sensed a comradery with the obscure blackness, as though he had found his true self, a safe place to reveal his desires. The music brought him understanding, acceptance, and purpose. He was content and confident that he would be led to the fulfillment of his destiny. For that, he was grateful.

***

The little pup lay within the confines of his steel prison, so weak and hungry he could barely emit a mere whimper. His small body ached from the burns, bruises, and whippings he had endured. His one escape was sleep, which he submitted to without hesitation. In his dreams, he could still remember that his name was Shermie. In his dreams, he found himself in the arms of his beloved person. He licked her chubby cheek, then her nose, and delighted in the squeals of laughter as she swatted him away with her tiny hand. "I love you," said the child in his dream.

Chapter Seventeen
The Battle Begins

Wayne Marshall sat at the kitchen table, overlapping the large bars of Shredded Wheat in his bowl with spoonfuls of warm milk until they were the desired squishiness. He knew Ozzie found humor in his intricate, precise habit of rearranging his food, mixing potatoes with vegetables, mashing the carrots in a stew, but Wayne had always thought it a perfectly reasonable practice. He'd have to ask Angela if she thought it was a compulsive behavior.

Look to the doctor. When all hope is gone, she will keep you strong.

Milk-covered bits of cereal flew from his mouth as he lunged forward, stunned. He hadn't mentioned it to Dr. Frank, but for the last week he'd begun hearing voices in his head, and not always pleasant ones. He wanted to speak to the doctor or Ozzie, but feared the outcome. The first time it happened, he was in the twilight stage just before falling asleep.

Sleep well my friend, for you have much to accomplish. Do not allow your fears to distract from your work ahead.

He'd passed it off as his vivid imagination or perhaps a daydream, until it happened again. The second time, the voice was far less kind and tender. It scared him so much he didn't want to think of it and pushed the memory back each time it popped into his head. He could feel it lurking in the recesses of his mind, waiting and watching. Wayne held it off for a day or two but then eerie, horrendous music filled his head and remained, continuing its constant tone of doom and despair. If not for the soft, perfectly chorded melody that had increased in volume to drown out the ugly sounds, he believed he would have lost his mind. The beautiful music was followed by a rich, sweet, loving voice, soothing his fear, reassuring him of his sanity. The night before, all music had stopped, but now here it was again. Wayne wondered what it meant. *And why me?*

Angela was due in an hour and he hadn't performed the exercise she prescribed in the last three days. Gathering his courage, he walked to the front door, stopped, and stared through its small oval window. Fighting back panic, Wayne thrust open the door, a rush of warm air hitting his face and stepped outside, one foot, then the other.

He closed his eyes and filled his lungs with air. *Okay, enjoy the smells of the honeysuckle, roses and green grass. Do what the doctor said. I'll be fine. Easy now. Get accustomed to the feeling of openness. Hear the sounds of animals, neighborhood children, and cars driving by. Remember, I am safe, no one will harm me. There's no need to give in to anxiety.* Wayne relaxed and opened his eyes to survey the row of houses to his right, his neighbor Zelda carrying a large bag of groceries through her front entrance, and a silver Prixa making its way toward the corner stop sign.

Now it was merely a matter of opening up the front gate and walking through it. He was calm as he neared the fence, filled with assurance he had no worry or fear. Taking a deep breath, he carefully lifted the gate's latch, hearing the clicking sound of metal releasing, and confidently walked through, finally able to exhale.

Without warning, Wayne was pushed back through the gate with such force he toppled to the ground, his face sliding through the thickness of the grass into the stones and debris beneath. As he lay gasping for air and trembling in shock, his body was lifted and thrust back through the open door of his home. Lying on his back in the avocado-tiled entranceway, he attempted to make sense of what was happening to him. A mass of darkness appeared, emanating a baleful presence of evil.

The cloud of malevolence descended, choking off Wayne's scream of horror.

Part III

CONFLICT EXPLORED

Appearance, a façade of who one seems to be
Therein lurks a different view
our eyes do not perceive
Protective covers engulf the tales of life experience
which form the core of acts and deeds
performed by any man
Lift each layer to reveal truth of lessons learned
memories so long suppressed
flow forth in utter clarity
each vision unadorned

~Monica M Brinkman, 2014

Chapter Eighteen
Jared's Revelation

Jared sat at his desk, reflecting on the strange malfunction of both microphone and guitar. One time, yes, that would be an accident, but twice in such a short amount of time, well, that was no coincidence. But why? And who? He knew it was a given that every politician has enemies but, shit, he was starting to eye everybody he saw with suspicion. So far, the authorities had no leads.

He leaned forward in the chair and pressed the intercom, "Yolanda"

"Yes, Governor," came the monotone reply.

"I'm feeling under the weather. I'll be going home in a minute. Don't schedule any future engagements or meetings until I give you the okay."

"Yes, sir. I understand. Wait a sec." Jared could hear the clicking of keyboards. "Jared, you have a meeting with Representative Foster tomorrow morning. Do you want me to cancel it?"

"Please. And thank you for bringing it to my attention. I'll be leaving shortly."

"Hope you feel better, sir."

"I'll call you." Jared clicked off the intercom and left his office, ready to find sanctuary within his home, prepared to sort out reality and reason from what had become madness.

***

He slid back through the carved wooden door, being careful to close and lock it tight behind him. After setting the alarm, he knew he had mere seconds to make his escape. His eyes solemn, his intentions great, he looked to the street and his surroundings, making certain he was undetected before walking to his vehicle, intentionally parked two blocks away.

***

He couldn't wait to get into his robe and slippers and relax. It had been quite a while since he'd taken time off from his job as governor. In fact, Jared felt a bit guilty doing so now, but fatigue mixed with fear gave him no alternative. Until he could figure out what was going on, he was not going to make any significant decisions for the people of his state. "Jared", whispered an unfamiliar voice, "do not give in to their power.

Remember who you are, not what you have become."

Caught off guard, he veered to the right of the roadway, barely missing a bicyclist. Sweat ran down his face *"That was much too close."* He steadied his grip on the steering wheel, intent on taking back control.

The welcoming sight of his residence came into view. He pulled into the four-car garage, shut off the engine, and sat while his body released some of its tension. At last, he was safe, a good feeling, and one he hadn't experienced for days.

Entering the kitchen from the garage, he called, "Elaine, honey, I'm home." He heard shuffling and low voices coming from above and hurried up the stairs. The noise seemed to be coming from Elaine's bedroom. He cautiously approached her closed door and opened it quietly. Jared gasped at the sight of a naked Elaine assisting a bare-chested, disheveled young man step into his trousers. Suddenly aware of Jared's presence, the man picked up his shoes and rushed out of the room. Jared could hear rapid footsteps descending the stairs followed by a loud slamming of the front door. Jared turned to Elaine, who was fumbling to secure the sash of her white silk Prada bathrobe. He discovered he was actually more than a little amused to see his wife in such an uncomfortable situation and determined not to make it any easier on the normally poised and confident Elaine.

In a controlled whisper, Jared said, "So it has come to this, has it, dear wife. Where'd you find that one, the high school? It's not that I care one way or the other, but in our own home, Elaine. Why bring him here? Why would you do this to me?"

Elaine shook her head. "It just happened, Jared."

"I'm going to say this once and then we will never speak of it again. You are never, ever to bring your sexual encounters into my home again. I have a reputation to maintain and if word of this got loose, it could ruin my career. Do you understand?"

"I understand perfectly. Your home. Your reputation," she hissed. "You find me with another man and that's all you can think of, what people will say about *you*. It's all about you Jared; always has been."

"About me?" Jared sneered. "That is far from the truth, my darling wife, and you know it. Where is my heir? Where is our child?"

"We've been through this repeatedly, Jared. If you want an heir, we can adopt. There are so many needy children."

"Elaine, why is that so important to you?

Elaine pushed his hand away, stared out the balcony window, and shrugged, "As if you care. You'll simply mock me as you've done every other time I've voiced an opinion."

"Listen well to the whispers in the wind for therein lays the truth of your loved ones heart," came the clear, strong voice. The words touched

something deep inside him.

Had he been so wrong all these years? He had thought his wife selfish and self-absorbed, caring only for her looks and the riches he could bestow upon her. Could he be the one who was self-centered, giving no credence to her wishes? Had he pushed her into the arms of other men?

Jared rose, walked to where she stood, and asked, "Explain to me why adoption is this important to you, Elaine. I promise I won't insult or ridicule your words."

Elaine's heart warmed to the man standing before her as she remembered the person she'd loved for so long before fame had overtaken his life. And she thought about her friend Sissy.

"When I was little, Mother and Father made it an annual tradition to visit the local soup kitchen on Christmas Eve. One particular year, I was bundled into the limo, dressed in my finest red silk dress, the one with faux rabbit fur at the cuffs and hem. I expected, as on Christmas Eves past, a night of mingling with the poor. To my surprise, we drove through an elegantly carved steel-gated entrance, up a winding road and stopped in front of a building whose sign read American Children's Home – Emergency Care.

"Carrying an assortment of brightly wrapped presents, my father rang the doorbell. Heavy footsteps approached, and a woman I'd later learn was named Mary Johnston opened the door and greeted us with a stern look.

"'Wipe those feet on the mat before coming in. I have enough work to do without needing to wash this hallway again. Hurry up; you're getting the winter cold inside and Lord knows we can barely afford the heat bill as it is.'

"I went inside, clutching mother's hand. As my eyes adjusted to dim light, I could see the weathered wooden walls and freshly mopped linoleum floor. I followed Mother to a massive dining room where children sat at long wooden tables. I'm guessing there were about thirty or more of them.

"Father and Anderson, our chauffer, followed shortly after, bundles of packages piled high, hiding their faces as they carefully set the brightly wrapped gifts along each side. Voices rose in excitement, only to be silenced as Mrs. Johnston shushed them. She beckoned me and my parents to the front of the room and introduced us to the wondering, wide-eyed children.

"That's when it happened. There was this small, thin girl off to the left side of the last table on the right. At the exact moment I spotted her, she raised her head and looked directly into my eyes."

It was then that a life-long connection was forged; one that would last until the foster system destroyed Sissy. Even now, all these years later,

Elaine fought back tears.

"Stupid, misguided Sissy took her life at sixteen after one too many foster care rapes.

"When I heard the news, I swore I'd never bear a child of my own, but rather give all my love to one in need of a home. I made my vow not just to honor Sissy, but also with the hope that maybe one day I'd be free of the guilt that surrounded her soul. Why didn't I see it coming? Why didn't I help?"

Jared pulled her into his embrace. She would tell him all about Sissy later. Hope ignited a passion long suppressed as Jared swept Elaine into his arms and carried her to their bed.

"Remember this day," whispered in his ear. He clicked off the side table lamp light and thought, "No problem." He knew in his heart he'd never forget this moment.

Chapter Nineteen
Fill My Head with Hair

"Shit," Alana screamed and fumbled for the faucet as the shower's icy stream blasted her shampoo-lathered hair and soap-covered body. She hadn't even wanted to wash her hair this morning, but she had a contract clause that said she had to try out the new line. Alana adjusted the water temperature and pulled the lever to full blast. The tepid water washed the suds from her hair and ran down her gardenia-scented body. Rinsed to her satisfaction, Alana stepped out of the shower, grabbing the thick beige towel from its hook on the bathroom door.

She turned toward the gold-edged full-length mirror hung on the inside of the door as she patted her body dry, bent forward and scooped her hair into the fluffy damp towel, piling it atop her head. Alana smiled, taking in the full scope of her body, a body that would soon be the envy of every teenage girl and young woman in the world. The idea of worldwide notoriety created excitement and stirred emotions of grandeur she had been longing to possess for years. It was well worth getting rid of that candy-assed Misty. Youthful Renewal deserved the best. Soon it would be her face spread across the world on magazine covers and in TV ads. She knew eventually film offers would follow; all she had to do was bide her time, smile, and look fantastic.

In bra and panties, she stuck her feet into white fluffy slippers and walked to the kitchen, where she grabbed a mug from the counter and poured a hot cup of freshly perked coffee. After adding half a spoonful of hazelnut coffee creamer to the steaming brew, she settled into the red painted metal chair that stood next to a matching square table, placed the mug on the tabletop, and pulled her legs close to her body, hugging them in her arms. She was proud of the smoothness and firmness of her legs. She stretched one out and reveled in the sensation of rubbing her hand down its length.

Her smug attitude was interrupted by an odd feeling in her scalp, at first just a slight twinge, but it was followed by an itch so strong she had to scratch. When she pulled her hand away from the affected area, she gasped in horror. Within her fingers coiled an abundance of shiny strands of her golden hair. She shook them off with violence, then jumped from her chair and raced to the hallway mirror. Stroking her hair, it quickly became apparent that something was very, very wrong—her hair was falling out. Her breath coming in short gulps, she peered closer into the mirror and saw a small bald spot on her forehead near her right temple. Alana touched the spot cautiously. It wasn't sore or tender to the touch, yet, as she pulled her finger away, a few more strands dropped to the floor. *What do I do?* If she didn't attend the show that evening, she'd be in breach of contract. *I need a doctor.*

***

Alana sat in the waiting room, tapping her right foot in nervous anticipation. She despised doctors and the way they invaded the most personal parts of a person's life. Not only did you have to go through the routine of being poked and prodded, but also they insisted on playing psychiatrist, always asking if you had any recent traumatic experiences or if you could be under some sort of stressful situation at home. She just wanted the exam over and done. More importantly, she needed a quick fix to her present hair loss crisis.

A heavyset young woman dressed in gray pants and a flower-print blue blouse opened the door to the waiting room and called out her name. Alana jumped up and followed her down the short hallway. After stopping to get her current weight, she was led to a tiny exam room and instructed to hop onto a white paper-covered steel table. The medical assistant wrapped the gray blood pressure monitor around her arm, told her to be still, and began pumping until satisfied she could get a proper reading. After a moment, the young assistant stated, "105 over 76, your blood pressure is fine." She wrote this down on a clipboard and asked, "What are you seeing the doctor for today Ms. Colbert"?

Christ, don't these people keep track of what you tell them when you make an appointment?

"I seem to have an issue with my scalp or hair. I've noticed strands are coming out at an alarming rate."

The assistant nodded as she wrote down the information. "The doctor will be with you shortly. I don't see the need to undress, so just sit tight."

Alana shivered and drew her hands to her elbows. It irritated her that they always kept these damn rooms so chilly and she wondered why, since most patients had to don those ridiculous white paper gowns. She wished he'd hurry up. She scanned the room seeking something, anything, to occupy her troubled mind, but there was nothing but the normal swabs, bandages, tissues, and medical posters. She swung her legs back and forth, letting out some of her growing tension. Her thoughts wandered to the event that night, and she was thinking about what clothes and accessories she would wear when a knock at the door followed by, "Ms. Colbert," jolted her back to the present. A middle-aged physician introduced himself as Dr. Levorawitz, peered over his black-rimmed glasses and sat in the metal, wheeled, brown round cushioned chair next to the exam table.

"So what seems to be the problem, Ms. Colbert"?

Here we go again. Didn't his fat-assed nurse write anything she told her down in the chart?

"I seem to be losing my hair."

"Is this the first episode or has it occurred previously?"

"Doctor, I have never had any problem with hair loss. In fact, I can truly boast that my hair has been one of my best features; not even a split end."

"Have you been under any emotional stress or changed your eating habits in any way"?

Alana sighed. She'd known this conversation would take place. "No, I haven't had additional stress, and I have been on a vegan diet for the last four years. In fact, I've experienced quite the opposite in my life. I could not be happier."

"Well, let's take a look." Dr. Levorawitz rose, pulled a pair of synthetic rubber gloves from the box that sat on the counter, stretched them over his hands, and stood next to the exam table. "Show me where you've noticed the most prominent hair loss."

Alana pulled the hair back from her forehead, exposing the balding area near her right temple.

Touching the afflicted area, he asked, "Does this hurt?"

"Not at all."

"There doesn't seem to be any redness or swelling to indicate an infection. I'm going to need to take some blood and urine samples and send them to the lab to rule out hormonal changes or disease. I'll have my nurse come in and we'll get back with you as soon as the test results come in."

"So what do I do in the meantime? I am a spokesperson for the Youthful Renewal line of cosmetics and beauty products, a very elegant, elite line, might I add. I certainly cannot be seen in public with bald spots on my head. I must look perfect at all times."

"Now, Ms. Colbert, I'm sure with your expertise you'll be able to camouflage it until we find out what's going on." He patted her hand in a fatherly way, smiled, and added, "I'll prescribe some medication that may help in preventing additional hair loss. It's vitamin based and we've seen some amazing results. My office will call you as soon as those tests come back."

The grimace on her face showed her dissatisfaction with his answer, but there was nothing she could do. She said, "Thanks, Doctor, but please be sure to call me the minute those tests are back."

"Will do." Dr. Levorawitz walked toward the door, stopped and looked back at his patient, and said, "Chin up. You're a lovely young woman, and I do understand why you're upset. I promise we'll find out what's going on."

Alana stopped focusing on how long it might take to get the test results back and concentrated on deciding what scarf she'd wear that evening to hide her imperfection.

Chapter Twenty
Misty's Encounter

Misty Lane had decided she'd had enough of wallowing in self-pity. It was time to look toward the future. She'd been drowning herself in booze, hiding from the world. She was suddenly ready to move on with her life. High on her priority list was getting her confidence back. The ability to once again trust others would come eventually, she hoped, but that could be the most difficult part. She'd been very trusting of both her boss, John Reynolds, and that conniving little witch, Alana Colbert. While she had no proof, Alana's sudden rise to fame was certainly suspicious. In retrospect, she remembered people giving her less-than-veiled warnings, advising her to be careful of the young woman. But she didn't see it. Now she felt ridiculous. She had believed Alana actually cared about her. She hadn't seen the betrayal coming, and that really hurt.

Just that morning, a magazine advertisement about a man named Monty Frank who held widely acclaimed seminars to assist those who were in need of self-esteem or financial assistance had caught her eye. Normally, she wouldn't attend a meeting like that. But it seemed there was another side to him, a humanitarian side. It seemed much more was addressed at the seminars than self-esteem. Her quick research revealed that they provided resources for the hungry, the homeless, and the mentally ill.

With her ego bruised and her self-confidence in the gutter, it was time to take positive action.

Misty walked up the stairs to retrieve her handbag. As she passed the glass mirror on the hallway wall, she stopped for a moment to study her reflection. What she saw distressed and shocked her. This stragglyhaired, naked-faced, unkempt woman in dirty pajamas was certainly not the person she wanted to present to the world.

Misty proceeded to her bedroom and poked around inside her purse until she found her cell phone. Pulling out the scrap of paper from the right pajama pocket, she dialed the number she'd jotted down. After it rang through, she was placed on hold, listening to a list of the venue's upcoming events.

"Good morning, Hilton San Francisco Financial District, how may I assist you?"

"Um, I read Monty Frank will be speaking at an event this evening and wondered if you still have any seats available."

"Let me check."

Misty could hear the click of the keyboard.

After a brief pause, the operator was back. "There are three seats left at the back of the room if you'd like one of them."

"Yes, please. Can you confirm the time and location of the room, please?"

"Seven p.m. in the Washington Room. When you enter, take the elevator to the second floor. It's the fourth room on the right. Do you want to confirm your attendance?"

"Yes, I do."

"We require payment via credit or debit card. May I ask which you will be using?"

Misty felt a twinge of excitement grow as she gave the clerk her name, address, phone and credit card information. It was as if a huge weight was off her shoulders. After hanging up she looked at the alarm clock atop her end table. Almost ten thirty. The way she looked right now, making herself presentable could take some time.

***

Monty Frank peeked into the Washington Room from behind the drape of the thick maroon stage curtain. "Full house tonight," he thought. And, as always, he was sure the evening would be a success.

A spot of hazy darkness in the air surreptitiously crept closer, wrapping its transparent arms around Monty's body, flitting back and forth, caressing his joyful face with dull, dim shadows of desolation. He stepped back as ice cold shivers ran across his body. Monty instinctively wrapped his arms around his torso, hands clutching his elbow. Maybe he should have the hotel staff check the air circulation crossed his mind, but he thought better of it, for the cool air would assist in maintaining the crowd's attention. A too-warm room put people to sleep. The house lights flickered on and off, causing a stir as people rushed to find seating.

He loved the Washington Room. It was more like a mini arena complete with raised stage, lush drapes, and small spotlights projecting from the finely crafted rafters. A small community theater had previously occupied the space and everything had been kept intact.

No matter how many times Monty spoke to an audience, nerves set in right before each gathering. Trying to appear nonchalant, he rubbed his sweaty palms against his pant legs and walked confidently to the podium. The house lights brightened, quieting the murmuring crowd. Monty scanned the room, happy to see a full house, tapped the microphone, and said, "Welcome."

After the expected round of applause, Monty began the well-rehearsed introduction of his program.

"I imagine most of you aren't here today because of my good looks or to hear yet another self-professed guru promise your life will change only if you purchase his recently released book. In fact, I don't want to sell you anything. Believe me, if that was my intention, all of you would have quite a bit of reading to do this evening. You see, at one time, I lived my life from a place of greed. Nothing was more fulfilling than the idea of bilking some idiot out of his or her hard-earned money. I'd play on their desperation, swearing I could solve financial woes if they'd just sign on the dotted line."

There were gasps of surprise at his words. Monty moved away from the podium and sat on the front edge of the stage, legs dangling freely as he looked into some of the many shocked faces before him. He smiled sweetly, nodding as he scanned the audience from left to right, ending in a focused stare toward the middle.

"Back then, money ruled my life. I woke up every day eager to reel in as many new clients as possible. I didn't care at all what it did to them. All that mattered was how much moola I could grab."

He paused for a moment, looking into the eyes of several members of the group, seeing the questioning shock he'd expected. Clearing his throat, he continued.

"Ah, yes, life was grand, it was. Money poured in. I had power and the thrill of control I held over others as I played the role of redeemer, never giving a thought to the impact my actions had in their lives. None of that mattered to me. I was a selfish, avaricious bastard who gloried in the adrenaline rush of each new conquest. Never satisfied, I longed for that next phone call or e-mail asking for advice or assistance." Monty's voice lowered to almost a whisper. "There was one small problem, though, known as 'the wife'."

His words brought the expected chuckles from the audience. Monty leaned forward. "You see, my beautiful, sweet, unsuspecting spouse knew none of the particulars of my job. I'd been able to hide the lengths I'd go to, the lies I'd tell, the false promises I'd make to people just like you."

He braced his right hand on the stage edge, swung one leg onto the floor and stood, turning his body away from the audience, then, in a swift turn, faced them again.

In a thunderous voice he stated, "When power goes to your head, it shuts off your heart."

Monty lowered his voice and said, "I thank my wife every day for forcing me to see the man I had become. Angela opened my eyes and I swore that I would spend the rest of my life helping people get out of their financial disasters or emotional issues."

"And that help, my friends, is what I'll be sharing with you this evening. There won't be any gimmicks, no false guarantees; just honest, proven ways to turn your life around."

A round of applause followed his words.

Misty Lane was impressed, although a bit wary of the self-admitted former con man. Was he speaking the truth or was this yet another carefully planned ploy? His seeming honesty sparked a decision to withhold judgment until she heard the entire speech. There was something different about him. Misty paid close attention to the rest of the presentation, even memorializing parts of it with her digital voice recorder. He was actually providing real tools and pertinent information about organizations that could help. And there was no mention of fees for the programs he talked about. It sounded like it would take some work and time, but that anyone could fix their situation without having to pay someone to help them. Even for those needing medical or emotional assistance, there were various options presented.

***

The darkness crept amongst the crowd in misty fingers of gloom and desolation, stealthily inserting emptiness and desperation into each soul it touched.

Chapter Twenty-One
Angela's Anguish

Her hand trembled as she put the phone down. What an odd call. She hadn't been expecting such a setback. Her last session with Wayne had gone extremely well. Now he was hearing demonic voices, experiencing hallucinations. And they'd started on his first attempt to leave the house.

Angela slung her purse over her shoulder and walked briskly to her car. The day was overcast, but a few rays of light peaked through the clouds as she slid into the car and started the engine.

His words haunted her. "It's got a hold on me, Doctor. I'm suffocating. Please help me, please, Angela, hurry." Whatever could he mean?

***

Wayne crouched in the master bedroom closet. His body shook as the ominous darkness taunted him with prodding touches upon his arm-covered head. Tears fell from his tightly closed eyes as he muffled a sob of hopelessness, beseeching, "Get away. Leave me alone. Please, I'm begging you."

Maniacal roaring laughter followed, bellowing through the air until Wayne broke down in weeping, wailing cries of fear. He had never been so scared in his entire life, not even when he was being beaten and thought he might die. This was real—at least to him—but it went against all reason and sanity. The darkness became a gloomy, foggy mass, encasing Wayne's body. The laughter grew impossibly louder, reverberating and echoing in the small space. Wayne could feel it seeping into him. He was helpless against the malevolent blackness. Without knowing it, he screamed.

***

She knew she was driving too fast, among other things, but she had to get to Wayne. Angela checked the rearview mirror as she turned the wrong way onto a one-way street. Just one more street to cross and she'd be there. Wheels screeching to a halt in front of Wayne's house, Angela jumped out of the car and ran to the front door. She knocked, waited for a few seconds, and then called, "Wayne? It's Angela. Let me in." She knocked again, at the same time trying the doorknob. To her surprise, the door was unlocked.

"Wayne, Wayne, are you here?" she called as she entered the house. "It's Angela, Wayne." She trotted down the hall, turning left into the first bedroom. "Wayne? Wayne?"

A pained cry from the closet startled her. Angela drew closer and opened the closet door. It took a moment for her eyes to adjust before she could make out the figure lying in a mound of clothing and fallen wooden hangers. She crouched beside him, not touching him for fear he'd been hurt and she'd cause further damage, and spoke softly, soothingly, hoping he'd respond.

"Wayne, it's Angela. Are you hurt? What's happening here?"

The body on the floor heaved a sigh of relief. "Thank God you've come." Raising his head, he looked into her face. "That thing, it attacked me. There was nowhere to hide. I tried. I tried with all my might but I couldn't fight it off. It was too strong."

"Wayne, let's get you out of this closet. I'll make some green tea and we'll talk. Okay." She patted his arm as she spoke.

Rising to his feet, Wayne stretched out his hand, which Angela took, steadying herself as she stood.

"I'll get the tea, Angela. It'll help to do something." He motioned Angela to sit at the kitchen table while he filled the teakettle. She noticed his hands quivered slightly when he placed the kettle on the stovetop. She didn't know what had happened, but it had certainly shaken him to the core.

Fight it.

She tried to ignore the voice in her head. Just what Wayne needed was for his shrink to go bonkers.

It is strong. It is evil. It can kill.

Wayne, carrying two cups of steaming tea in somewhat steadier hands, joined her at the table.

Flicking a stray hair from her face, Angela said, "So do you want to talk about what just happened? Do you feel up to it? I don't want to pressure you."

Wayne lowered his head. "Where do I begin? God, Doctor—I mean Angela—I don't even know how to explain it. You won't believe me anyway." He looked up, eyes pleading for understanding.

Angela said, "You have no idea what I'm capable of understanding. Give me a chance."

Taking her at her word, Wayne recounted what had happened. Angela stifled a gasp when he described the blackness that had descended upon his body and the powerful energy it created.

"It has arrived. Be prepared."

What she had most dreaded was coming to pass. Her eyes softened in

The Wheel's Final Turn

sympathy as she looked at her patient. "I believe you, Wayne. As someone who's seen things you could never imagine, I know what you say is true."

Wayne could hardly believe what he'd heard. She understood and believed him.

"If anything like this happens again, I want you to call me immediately. And I'm going to write you a prescription that'll help you relax. Oh, and for what it's worth, what happened to you is not related to your phobia."

"How's that, Doctor? I mean, what is this thing? Is it going to come back?"

"Wish I had the answer to that one, Wayne. I don't know whether it will or won't come again. But you can't let fear that it might run your life."

After writing the promised prescription and handing it to Wayne, Angela gathered her purse and started toward the front door. Wayne followed and opened it for her.

Angela gave him an encouraging smile. "You'll be fine. And, Wayne, promise you'll call me if anything strange happens. Promise?"

He nodded. "Promise." And watched her turn back toward the walkway, longing for her to stay, knowing she could not.

Chapter Twenty-Two
Hanky Panky

He hit the alarm clock so hard it flew onto the floor, cracking the plastic covering.

"Shitty God damned cheap piece of garbage."

Hank picked up the damaged clock, slammed it on the end table with such force it shattered into tiny pieces. He turned away from the mess and plopped onto the edge of his bed, scratched his balding head, stretched his arms, and belched. No time to fret over the clock; it was time to get ready for another day of work.

Dressed in Spider Man boxer shorts, he padded to the kitchen. Taking a large tan mug from the cupboard, he filled it with strong coffee. The silence of morning was irritating. It brought thoughts of guilt into his mind, right alongside ideas of violence. A constant fight ensued; the conflict throbbed inside his brain, creating such intense pain he felt surely his skull would burst. Hank grabbed the remote, pushed the button for Channel 5, and held the sound button until the news anchors voices drowned out the noise in his head.

He stared at the screen, his dark eyes blank and lifeless, unable to comprehend the meaning of the news anchors words. His leg draped over the other, his right foot shook in uncontrollable spasms, sending shocks of pain up his right leg. From the blackness came a voice that sliced through his consciousness. *I am the one, the keeper of your fate.*

Hank jumped to his feet, shook his head, and pounded with fisted hands at his ears. Spit dripped from the sides of his mouth and his heart pounded. One word repeated relentlessly: *Retsasid*. It grew louder and louder until he thought his eardrums would explode. He fell to his knees, hands cupping his forehead, and sobbed from deep within his soul. His head throbbed; his nerve endings twitched and burned until his body gave in to the enveloping pain and he collapsed onto the cold tile of the kitchen floor. He never knew sound could be so painful. All he could do was endure.

Retsasid, retsasid, retsasid.

The voice fell silent and Hank groaned with relief.

After lying still for a few minutes, he struggled to his feet. As he did, he caught a fleeting glimpse of a man's face through the kitchen window. Hank raced to the window, but saw no one. How could that be? Wrinkled face, graying beard, glaring eyes; he'd seen him plain as day.

Hank turned away, still a bit shaken. He grabbed a whiskey bottle from the cupboard, twisted off the cap, and took a long swallow. The bitterness and warmth of the liquor made him shudder, but he brought the bottle to his mouth and took another huge gulp.

Hank glanced at the coffeemaker's clock and realized that, unless he skipped shower and shave, he'd be late for work. "God damn it", he muttered. This day was turning into a piece of shit. He walked to the bedroom, found the clothes he'd worn the day before, and decided they'd have to do.

As he pulled the wrinkled plaid shirt over his shoulders and slid his arms into the sleeves, he felt a sharp flash of pain at his right wrist. *What the—* He grabbed at the leather bracelet in an attempt to rip it off, but it would not yield, tightening and sinking deeper into his skin. Hank stumbled to the dresser, slid out the small top drawer, and fumbled for his pocketknife.

"Son of a bitch," He screamed in agony as he released the sharp blade and slid it under the leather strap. As he sawed against it, each turn and twist of the blade brought pain so severe his eyes watered. Blood seeped from beneath the obdurate leather, bright red beads dropping onto the dense beige carpet beneath his feet.

Retsasid, retsasid, retsasid.

Chapter Twenty-three
A Big Commitment

Jared wished they'd check with him before booking any appearances. He'd forgotten all about McBride's voice mail last month. Good thing Sandra called to remind him that rehearsal would begin at three o'clock that afternoon. With everything that was going on with Elaine, it had completely slipped his mind. His PR staff had decided his image needed a boost with the younger crowd and had come up with this not-so-brilliant idea. The governor of California was going to appear before a crowd at the Oracle Coliseum. He'd give a grand speech and a bona fide musical performance. He hadn't played guitar to a crowd in over five years and now those idiots expected him to do so before the entire nation. Of course the press had been notified and invited, and the event would be plastered across the internet and major news stations.

He walked to the closet, opened the door, and lifted the guitar case from the darkened corner. His thoughts went to the last time he'd played. He hadn't taken the time to get old Blue in for repair. And now there wasn't time. All he could do was hope whatever electrical malfunction he'd experienced was a one-time thing.

"Damn it," he muttered as he left the bedroom, Blue in hand.

***

There was something special about their relationship, a bit of magic or perhaps shared intuition. Karman chuckled as she recalled Euclid's feeble attempts to hide his actions and the growing visions of what was to come. He should have realized that she, too, was getting signs from above.

Karman, follow his plan without question or doubt. Euclid is in our hands. He needs your support and unwavering faith. The darkness grows and it is amongst us.

Euclid still wasn't divulging much. She supposed there was no reason to say much of anything about his actions, other than to let her know when he wasn't going to be home for an evening. He knew she'd be there at his side whenever he required her assistance. It was her part of destiny.

***

As Jared pulled into the parking lot of the coliseum, he began to feel more relaxed and actually almost eager to get on stage. If there was a heaven on earth, playing music was it.

"Hi, guys, how's it going"? He walked up and set the guitar case on the stage floor.

"We'll be ready in a few, Mr. Williams," said the tech crew supervisor.

Jared walked to the young man and extended his hand. The man dropped the wires he was working on, wiped his hand on his faded blue jeans, and met the offer with a firm handshake.

"Oh, by the way, no need to be formal. Call me Jared, please."

"Name's Mike. Nice to meet you, Gov—I mean Jared. I'll have the stage ready in about fifteen minutes." Mike pointed to downstage left, "In the meantime, go grab yourself a cold one and relax."

"Thanks. Will do, Mike." Jared picked up the guitar case, and paused to look around. His staff was putting up political photos. There he was, face plastered across the room. He'd never gotten used to seeing his image in these gigantic posters. He supposed it was a necessity; after all, this was a fundraising event. What a shitty motto they'd come up with, though. Williams—Voice of Your Future.

Jared went backstage, set his guitar case down and walked to the white foam cooler. He reached inside, grabbed a Bud Light and pulled the tab off, lifting the cold metal to his mouth and downing half its contents. Nothing tasted as good as cold brew before a show.

There were a handful of people in the room. He figured the young women, one a skinny blonde and the other a large-breasted black woman with straight bobbed hair, were his backup singers.

Jared walked over to them. "Well, ladies, do you think we'll pull this rehearsal off without a glitch?" He smiled the broad, warm, toothy grin that had charmed woman all across the state.

The young blonde woman looked up. She had the deep, dark brown, almost black eyes. She nodded. "You got it, Governor. By the way, my name is Cynthia and this is Rhonda." She elbowed the beautiful tall bronze-skinned woman standing next to her. Rhonda giggled and gave him a high-five. "Yeah, got it down."

Mike stuck his head out from behind the massive curtains. "We're about ready to begin, folks. Need you three on stage in five minutes for a sound test."

Jared could feel the adrenalin pulse through his body as he walked onto the stage.

Of course, all the equipment had already been tested, except for Jared's guitar. He'd forgotten to leave it when he went backstage.

Mike said, "Hey, Jared, you want me to test that beautiful guitar? I'd be honored to do so."

The Wheel's Final Turn

Jared shook his head. "I'm fine, Mike. This baby almost tunes itself. Give me a minute."

His fingers strummed the strings and he then plucked each separately. As he'd figured, just a bit of minor adjustment was necessary.

"Okay, guys, I'm ready to make some music," he said after a couple of minutes.

The stage was completely dark. The lead guitar player led off with a soft, rapid rhythm of notes that grew louder as the lights came on, a white light spot shining on Jared. The bass player joined in. Jared strummed his first chords and began the song.

"Every man and woman, each awakening mind, needs a bit of courage to really change the times."

The gray-haired man watched the rehearsal from behind the stage. Bits of wood fell to the floor as he whittled. His timing had to be precise. He knew he could not get caught fiddling with Jared's guitar after the practice. He looked upward and shook his head. "Hey, voice. Ya better be with me and guide my hand."

I am always with you, came the swift response.

Part IV
REDEMPTION

Comes a time to pay the price
for how you chose to live your life
A caring heart may turn ice cold
if given silver, jewels, and gold

There are those so sweet and kind
 steadfast in will, and strong in mind
No amount of bribery
will alter generosity

Step right up and take a stand
Show your side across the land
Hidden secrets show their face
caring not of faith or race

The Wheel's a force of clarity
spinning through eternity
Can you face its scrutiny?
Open for the world to see

~Monica M Brinkman, 2015

Chapter Twenty-four
Monty's Ordeal

"Sweetie, how're you feeling?"

Monty turned onto his side. He wondered if he should tell Angela the truth. He felt like shit. Ever since the last conference his head wouldn't stop pounding and his thoughts were once again focused on acquiring great wealth. He had visions of himself giving a lecture holding large canvas bags filled with hundred dollar bills, so full the cash overflowed and fell onto the stage as he moved and spoke to the audience. It petrified him. He decided to keep quiet about it. Surely it would pass.

He tried on a smile, "Much better, Ang."

Monty knew he had to act as normal as possible. He lunged toward her with playful enthusiasm, caught her around the middle and pulled her slender body on top of his. Putting his finger under her chin, he drew her mouth to his and they shared a long passionate kiss.

Angela drew her head back and smiled. "I'd say you certainly are feeling much better."

She laughed and swatted away his hand as he reached for her breast.

"Not now, babe. Gotta get dinner ready for the twins. Give me a rain check?"

"You got it. I could use some food, too."

Truth was, Monty was relieved. He felt about as passionate as a pot of noodles. *Damn this headache!* Aspirin, codeine, nothing worked. He turned to his side and hugged the fluffy pillow, attempting to find a comfortable position. After a few minutes he realized that the ache in his head was gone, replaced by a rumbling, bass-toned word.

Retsasid. Retsasid, retsasid, retsasid.

The sound intensified until it roared in his mind. He covered his ears, closed his eyes, and threw his head from side to side. After what seemed an endless time, the word was replaced by hysterical laughter.

Monty opened his eyes to find that the once bright sunlit bedroom had grown dark. It smelled of rotted flesh. The stench filled Monty's nostrils and he suppressed the urge to gag.

Retsasid, retsasid, retsasid.

"Dear God, help me," he sobbed through trembling lips and rolled from the bed to the carpeted floor with a loud thud. There was no release, no place to hide. Monty resisted with all the power he could muster.

"No! I will never allow you within my soul. You will not take me again!"

His voice could be heard even in the kitchen

"Mommy, it's Daddy," cried Alexis. Alicia rushed to her sister's side and held her in a tight embrace.

"What's wrong with him, Mom?" Alicia was unable to hide her alarm.

"It's all right, girls. Daddy's just having a bad dream."

Angela ran up the stairs and into the bedroom where she saw her husband curled on the floor, holding his ears, tears streaming down his anguished face. The unexpected darkness of the room told her the evil was back.

She rushed to his side, knelt, and lifted his head onto her lap.

"Oh, Monty, sweetie, I'm here. It's okay. It's Ang."

He looked up and Angela saw the fear etched upon his face and in his eyes. She smoothed his brow, wishing, she could make it all go away. Their eyes locked and no words were necessary. They knew the darkness had returned.

"It won't stop, Ang. I can't stand it any longer."

"What, Monty? What won't stop? Tell me."

"Retsasid! Don't you hear the voice? This damned crazy voice keeps repeating it over and over and over again. Retsasid. What does it mean?"

Anger flared. So this is how it was going to be.

"You listen to me, Monty. Don't you see, there is no voice that can hurt you. Do *not* allow it to take control. It is the blackest of all evils. Fight it, damn it. You have to fight back." She took his hands in hers. "Together, we will end this wickedness. Look into my eyes, Monty."

He turned away.

"Do it," she demanded.

Angela turned his face toward hers, held it in place, and fixed her eyes on his. She could smell the stench of all the evil in the world, all the greed and violence, and, most of all, she could smell the destruction and death. She could see the blankness in his eyes.

"Monty, listen to me. Think of goodness, love, peace." She put her lips to his ear and whispered, "You *must* fight back."

Angela thought only of grace, of lightness and joy as she resumed staring into Monty's eyes. Finally, saw the blankness ebb. She did not release her hold on him until the brightness of life appeared in his eyes once more.

The light of day filled the room. The darkness had been vanquished.

Monty put his arms around her and they rocked in a soothing rhythm of love until he relaxed and grew drowsy. Angela released her hold.

"It's gone Monty. Let's get you into bed. I'll come back with a sandwich and maybe some fruit in a while. Right now, you need to rest."

She helped Monty to his feet and he climbed into bed. Angela pulled the covers up and tucked them around him.

"Stay with me, Ang." His eyes pleaded.

Before she could answer, "Mommy, is Daddy all right?" Alicia called from the foot of the stairs.

Angela got up and walked to the top of the stairs and looked down into the questioning face of her daughter. "Yes, sweetie. Mommy will be down in a minute."

She hurried back to Monty and said, "I need to get back downstairs. We *cannot* allow this force to take over our lives. I promise, I'll be back to check on you soon."

He nodded his understanding. As she left the bedroom, Monty wondered if he had the strength to fight. He'd forgotten how strong a hold the darkness held upon its prey.

Memories flooded back. Angela had spoken of impending peril, but he'd chosen to ignore the negative and concentrate on their new life and his career. He'd only half-believed her warnings, anyway, and preferred to focus on reality. He realized now that he had made a mistake in underestimating the power of their adversary.

"May God help us all," he whispered. Exhausted in both body and mind, he fell into a much-needed sleep.

***

Angela hurried down the stairs and into the kitchen. The twins, seated at the red metal table, searched her face.

Always-sensible Alicia was the first to speak. "Was it a dream, Mother?"

Alexis chimed in, "Is he okay?"

"Your father is fine."

Angela walked behind her daughters and pulled them into her arms, kissing the tops of their heads.

"We've all had nightmares, right?" The twins nodded in agreement. "Daddy's really tired from all the business trips and I think his imagination got away from him. He just needs some rest."

"Yeah, Alish, remember that awful dream you had the other night? Something about being trapped in the dark? I had to shake you three times to get you to wake up. Boy, was you scared."

Alicia glared at her sister.

"Alicia, you had a dream about darkness?" Angela struggled to keep the alarm from her face and voice. This was not something she had expected.

Alicia shrugged her shoulders and flicked a stray piece of hair from her forehead. "It was only a dream, Mom. I'm okay." She picked up her fork and scooped a small bite of coleslaw into her mouth. Her mother had a faraway look in her eyes.

Alexis noticed it, too. "Mom, what's wrong?"

"Alex, it's nothing. I was just daydreaming. Now eat."

Alexis heard an odd tone in her mother's voice, and was pretty sure her mother was concealing something. She knew better than to push for answers; Mom would hide her worries, not wanting to upset anyone. But she was convinced that the physical world was different; there was a definite change. The atmosphere seemed denser, more silent, and more introspective. She decided that she, too, would hold her tongue until the moment was right to confront her mom. For now, she, concentrated on eating the bowl of pear slices, berries, and cream set before her.

Alicia caught her mother's eye and they shared a mutual look of understanding. She turned away, silent, deep in thought. She knew things, things her mother tried to keep secret. Like the time she'd overheard her talking to Karman about visions she'd seen and voices she'd heard. What her mother didn't know was that she also had experienced those same things. At first, she'd thought there was something wrong with her; that she was weird or even crazy. It brought her some relief to know someone else had the same experiences.

Alicia wished she were more like her sister. Alexis never had bad dreams or visions of doom. Her life was one of curiosity and adventure. On occasion, she felt foolish relating her thoughts to Alex. She'd read that twins can sense each other's emotions, but in this family, she seemed to be the only one who had paranormal experiences.

What worried her was that the darkness seemed to be growing, getting stronger, expanding into the crevices and corners of not only space but also minds. How much time did she have left before it took her over?

Chapter Twenty-five
Alana's First Event

Alana stood before the crowd and smiled. A standing ovation. She had finished her pitch on the latest Youthful Renewal line and they'd loved her. For once in her life, she felt important and validated for not only her beauty but also for her intelligence. And the scarf she'd chosen to wear to cover her hair loss had done its job. She was surprised that so many women—fashion experts and hairstylists—had complimented her on her new look. She'd pulled the zebra-print cloth over her entire scalp and tied it to one side, allowing the long ends to freely flow to mid-body. Now woman wearing similar scarves would soon be plastered over the cover pages of every best-selling beauty magazine. People were such fools. If only they knew her true reason for adopting her new look.

The crowd quieted to silence. Alana surveyed her audience.

"Wow, what a great reception. You have no idea how much I appreciate your support as the new spokeswoman for the best beauty product in the world, Youthful Renewal." She paused as a round of applause filled the room. "Thank you so much. I am truly flattered. It gives me great pleasure to have the privilege to represent such a fine organization, and even more to see so many of you in love with our product. To show our gratitude, we're holding a reception in the Silver Leaf room, so please join us for some refreshment."

Alana bowed her head, curtsied, and exited the stage while the audience once again gave her a standing ovation. The night was electric and it was her time to shine.

John Reynolds grabbed her shoulder, took her arm in his, and, with a broad smile, said, "Good girl. Very well done. Congratulations. I think you've got a long, bright future with us. Now it's time for our new star to mingle."

Alana suddenly felt the thrill she'd felt at her obvious success and at his praise be replaced by an almost overwhelming sense of despair. *Retsasid, retsasid, retsasid* echoed the voice in her mind.

***

Misty sat in the back center back row. She sniffled and brushed the tears from her eyes. She'd had to come, no matter how much it hurt—and it did—to see someone else so easily accepted in the role she had played for years. The public and press had proved once again to be fickle, quickly forgetting her name. All those loyal fans gone in an instant. Now that she'd seen for herself, perhaps she could put that chapter of her life away and begin anew. She supposed Monty Frank would have approved of her attendance this evening. She could hear him saying, "Face your past and let it go. Until you do that, you will never be free to reach your next goal."

Misty waited until the audience had thinned, then stood, brushed the creases from her skirt, and scooted to the aisle. Not really paying attention, she turned smack into the shoulder of a bearded, gray-haired man wearing an angler's cap.

"Oh, I'm so sorry. I wasn't looking."

The man raised his right eyebrow and grinned, steadying her with his hands. "No apology needed, ma'am. Not often an old geezer like me gets a chance ta say howdy to such a pretty young lady as you." He tipped his hat, extended his arm toward the exit. "After you, missy."

"Thank you." Misty smiled.

As they exited the building, her heart filled with unexpected peace. She could swear she heard someone whisper, "Look forward, for a new world awaits you."

***

Alana was happy to be home and get the damned scarf off. Her head itched. She'd had to resist the urge to scratch all night. She ripped it from her head and tossed it on the end table. Her fingers found their way to her scalp and she was finally able get some relief.

She turned on the bathroom light and peered into the mirror. Her eyes widened in horror. Where once hung glorious blonde tresses were patches of raw, oozing scalp. The red rash had traveled down the left side of her neck. She pulled the strap of her dress away to see that it had spread onto her shoulder, as well. She grabbed one of her few remaining locks of hair and screamed when it pulled away, stuck between her fingers.

"What am I going to do?" It was too much to process. "What should have been the best day of my life is turning into a nightmare." She took a deep breath and continued her out-loud conversation with herself. "Okay Alana, you can make this work. You have wigs, lots of wigs. You will get through this."

A smoky haze was slowly filling the room, irritating her eyes. It soon turned to blackness, hiding the glow of the overhead light. One by one, the round decorative bulbs around her mirror burst, pop, pop, pop, and small bits of glass stuck into her upper chest and face. She was bleeding and in complete darkness.

The Wheel's Final Turn

Alana raced to the sanctuary of her bedroom. She flung herself upon the bedspread, its pattern of pink roses and green leaves for once failing to comfort her, and sobbed with grief. Her looks were gone.

"Oh, no," she cried. The rash had spread to her arm and more of her hair lay atop the bedspread. Her lips were swollen and her cheeks puffed to double their size. She watched in terror as the darkness infiltrated the bedroom, unable to move as it pulsed slowly, steadily toward her. She could feel it touch her with its cold, damp density. A foul odor filled her nostrils. The room was freezing.

Alana's heart rate increased and her breathing became rapid. She begged, "No, please don't hurt me."

Guttural laughter filled the room. *Retsasid, retsasid, retsasid.* She shrieked, pulling away from the cold fingers touching her cheeks and hid her head under the thin pillow. She cringed in repulsion at each caressing stroke, her body involuntarily jerking away as the freezing touch traveled down her back. Her body trembled in fear and she sobbed in helplessness.

Retsasid, retsasid, retsasid. That was all she could hear.

"Dear God, somebody help me. Please help me. Help me. Help me. I promise to be good. I swear. Just make it go away."

Daring to peek from beneath the pillow, she saw a bright light. Turning her head to get a better view, she was surprised to see the figure of her grandmother Donia. Brilliant light surrounded Grandma's body, sending rays of iridescent gold and white beams of light into the room's blackness. The rays pulsated, growing larger with each throb. Grandma Donia's face glowed, her eyes were serene, and her lips were curved in an understanding smile. Alana raised her hand and placed it palm over her eyes to shield them from the radiance.

"Grandma, is that you? Have you come to help me? Have I died?"

The shape gracefully floated to Alana's side of the bed. It altered from near transparency to solid form, leaving no doubt in Alana's mind that it was her Grandmother Donia. The specter pulled the covers away from Alana's body and rubbed its hands across the young woman's neck, down her back, and onto her legs. Alana felt the chill of the room replaced by comforting warmth as the darkness's power waned. The deafening *retsasid* was gone. Her body ceased quivering and she felt a wonderful inner calm replace her terror.

Alana tossed the pillow to her side and sat, legs pulled to her chest, chin resting on her knees.

"Oh, Grandma, you saved my life. Thank you." She moved to embrace the figure. With a gesture of her hand, Donia shooed her away.

"Let me hold you, Grandma. I miss you so much."

The golden-lit figure sat upon the bed and took her granddaughter's hands in hers. She stared into Alana's eyes and spoke for the first time. Her voice was soothing, but held a direct firmness of intention. "My dear child, I have watched over you since my departure and you have grown into a stunning young woman. However, beware, my dear, for beauty is so much deeper than appearance. I fear you are now experiencing the results of years of deception, deceit, jealousy and self-indulgence."

Alana hung her head in shame, for what Grandma spoke was truth. "Child, look at me now."

Alana sensed the urgency and authority in Grandma Donia's voice. She raised her head. Alana's eyes reflected her feeling of ignominy. She knew better than anyone how disgraceful her actions had been.

"You are fortunate indeed. I have permission to make my presence known and interfere with the evil that is taking place, not only within your life, but also throughout the world. Today you experienced only a small bit of its powerful control."

"So you're real? This isn't my imagination?"

"Am I real, child?" Donia chuckled. "Ah, who knows what reality truly is, but, yes, it is I in the form you best remember. Now hush, for my time and energy is limited and must not be wasted on idle chitchat. There are things I must say, and, if you are wise, you will heed my words."

"But, Grandma, I don't understand what's happening to me."

"Soon it will be revealed to you. You must learn what is important and meaningful in life. Number one being the planets do not revolve solely around Alana, they rotate around all."

That statement stung. Alana hated to admit it, but it was fact. Her mind took her back to a time when life was not so perfect. A rush of long forgotten memories surfaced.

"You make me sound just horrible, Grandma. Don't you remember how it was before? I was mocked, teased, and tormented, all for a stutter I could not control. Do you call that fair? I was only a little girl and all I ever wanted was to be accepted. I think I would have killed myself if not for you. In fact, I know it."

The spirit nodded her head. "Of course I know of these things Alana. Think about this. Is stuttering the worst thing that could have happened in your life? Did teasing kill you? Or, perhaps, did it give you the fortitude and strength to use your intelligence? Why do you choose to carry those memories with you and allow them to change your heart?"

Alana pondered for a moment and then said, "I never thought of it that way. So what happens now?"

Donia turned her head away. "You have been given a choice and a great challenge. Let your heart and soul guide you."

Then she was gone.

"Come back, Grandma," cried Alana. "I don't understand."

The Wheel's Final Turn

Alana flung her body back against the bed and looked up at the ceiling. She absentmindedly twirled a lock of hair between her fingers only to have it fall from her head. Her hair was still falling out.

"Damn it."

Retsasid, retsasid, retsasid.

It was back. She could hear the rumbling of distant thunder as the atmosphere in the room once again grew thick with haze. Her head jerked to one side and her body lifted from the bed. With each cry of pain, the darkness grew blacker and more powerful as her agony fed its monstrous appetite.

Alana's head hit the bedpost and she heard a cracking sound. She was dizzy and her mind was foggy. Her Grandmother Donia's voice whispered in her ear, "The choice is yours."

Alana knew she could not fight the darkness with strength; she was no match against the evil. But what choice? Why hadn't Grandma told her? Then she remembered. *Let your heart and soul guide you.* She hadn't opened her heart since she was a little child and didn't know if she had the ability to do it now. She looked up toward the ceiling and said, "If there is any goodness or love for me, I beg you to send your power to me now. I cannot fight this darkness without your love surrounding me."

A voice cut through the darkness, "Go to the one called Angela. You will find her in the city of San Jose in Guadalupe Park. Your heart will take you there."

The malevolent black attacked the light carrying the words, suffocating it until it was no longer visible. Thunder roared and lightning zigzagged across the room, tearing into the dresser, splitting it in two, and releasing puffs of gray and white smoke that mixed with and became part of the darkness.

Chapter Twenty-six
The Color of Black

He closed the front door and walked to his studio. He pulled the cell phone from his pocket and dialed. He'd have Ozzie pick up the prescription Angela had written. His call went to voice mail after several rings, so he left a detailed message.

Wayne was sure Angela would be pleased to know he wasn't going to let what had happened get him down. He was plunging into his painting, in the hope that getting engrossed in work might be the best medicine.

But what to paint? He'd grown weary of catering to the style expected of him. He decided it was time to let the creative juices flow and see what poured from his imagination.

The darkness waited beside the doorway. Flicks of ebony caressed the frame. Despite its urgent desire to engulf its prey, it entered the studio with prudence, stealthily making its way to the far corner of the sunlit room, impatient to overcome the soul of the delicate young man and smother the splendor within his heart.

Wayne allowed his hands to direct the placement of the paint. The rich hue of Prussian blue glistened from the grey primed background. He unconsciously hummed a half-remembered ditty from childhood. The brushes caressed the canvas. Focused solely on his project, Wayne's mind released all restraints, allowing him to become lost in the joy of pure creation. His eyes were slightly unfocused as, emotionless, the expression of his inner vision was created through the movement of brushes layering paint without plan or preparation.

The darkness inched forward, low to the floor and unnoticed. As it reached Wayne, fingers of blackness formed that darted forth and entered his body, his heart, and his soul.

The brush hit the canvas with controlled vengeance, smearing globs of purple, brown, and gray onto the painting, covering Wayne's intentions with its own. His hands worked feverishly and sweat poured down his face as he continued the hectic pace. Hours merged into minutes, minutes into seconds, until there was no sense of time.

Satisfied, the darkness eased its grip and flowed out from the body it had commanded. Wayne, exhausted, his clothing soaked with sweat, fell to the floor. He looked up to view his masterpiece and stared in wide-eyed, mouth-gaping shock. Before him was the most ghastly, terrifying, monstrous creature he'd ever seen. He shrank from its evil glare and covered his eyes, yet he had to look again.

As he lay there, mesmerized by the figure on the canvas, memories he'd hidden for decades resurfaced.

***

He sat, a boy of seven, flipping through the pages of the magazine he'd found that morning, hidden in the attic among old books and records. Unaware of his true sexual orientation, all Wayne knew was he liked looking at the pictures of the men. The voice of his father interrupted his pleasure.

"Where did you get that disgusting rag?" his father barked, tearing it from his hands. "What are you, a pansy? This is filth, you hear me? No son of mine is going to be gay. I don't ever want to see you with this piece of garbage ever again. Understood?"

Wayne cowered in fear and humiliation. He didn't understand what he had done wrong as he watched his father remove the thick brown belt from his pant loops. His father approached him, saying, "This will hurt me more than it will you, son. I want you to remember this day."

The belt hit his back with force and he cried out in pain. Whack, whack, whack, continued the brutal beating, hitting arms, legs and chest. He started to cry, which angered his father even more.

"Stop that crying this minute if you know what's good for you or I'll give you something to really cry about."

After his father left, Wayne finally let himself cry. He loved his father and didn't understand why he'd become so angry over a magazine. He'd never heard the word gay and wondered what it meant. And if he didn't know what it meant, how was he supposed to keep from being it?

***

At thirteen, Wayne and Mike were best buddies. More than that, they shared something that had grown over their four-year friendship, something he dare not let his family know about.

His father was right. Wayne *was* gay, though he preferred the word homosexual. He and Mike were lovers, but kept it a secret. People, especially his school peers, were not always accepting.

A quick kiss behind the bleachers. A light flashed simultaneously with a water-filled balloon hitting him across the cheek. He and Mike looked in the direction of the flash and saw Dennis Wilderman running, camera in hand, toward his friends Butchie and Remy. They were pointing and laughing.

"Hey, fags, you want more of that?" Butchie hollered.

Mike shook his head and sighed. "Jerks. Come on, let's get out of here."

As the memory played on, Wayne saw his younger self waving goodbye to Mike and trudging the two and a half blocks to his own home. As he went through the front door, he found his father and mother standing in wait. His dad held something in his hand that he threw at Wayne's feet. Wayne reached down and picked it up. It was a color photo, a close-up of the kiss behind the bleachers.

His father walked to him, took hold of his front shirt and pulled him near, face to face. There was no mistaking the look of disgust in his father's eyes or the rage in his voice as he said, "Pack your stuff and get the hell out of here. You're dead to me. I have no son."

Wayne had never seen his father again.

***

Thunderous laughter rippled through the blackness.

***

The pain was fresh, as though memory was a reality he was living at that very moment. More visions of the past flashed before him, and more, all so hurtful his heart ached.

He heard a faint whisper. "Wayne, be not frightened."

He sat upright and listened.

I am with you always to lead the way. You have felt me through your artwork and carried me in your heart. The darkness has stolen your soul. Follow my command and I promise to stay by your side. Ignore me and you shall face the depths of despair.

"Who are you?"

I am the creator of all, the father of time and the voice of eternity.

"Are you God?" Wayne looked above him, seeking answers.

If that is what you wish, then I am so.

Wayne heard a rumbling from across the room and saw the darkness inching toward him. His half-mad mind tried to comprehend. He hesitated, then asked, "What do you want of me? I'll do anything you say."

Be at the Gardens of Discovery. I will come to you and guide you when the time is right. Until then, I wish you strength of conviction.

In one swoop, the evil was upon him, covering him with the madness of the damned and the taste of destruction.

Retsasid.

Chapter Twenty-Seven
About the Pup

Hank's derangement was complete. He descended the wooden stairs, still dressed in his bloody plaid shirt, his eyes glazed and staring. His ears buzzed. *Retsasid*. He moved closer to the cage, approaching with caution. There was a good chance that the starving animal had gone mad.

The small pup lay in a pile of excrement, his fur matted, his body limp, and his spirit broken. One ear perked when he heard the sound of the man drawing near. His heart pounded rapidly.

The cage door creaked as it opened and the man entered. He lay motionless, yet aware.

"Hey, fella, you sure look like hell."

Hank grinned as he pulled the pocketknife from his back pocket. He was anxious to perform the act. He'd been waiting for this moment since his captive's arrival. When they ceased yelping and barking, he had other ways to bring himself satisfaction. He walked to the pup and knelt down beside him. One hand held the dog's face down into the soiled floor, while the other held the sharp knife. He made his first cut to the thigh, laughing maniacally at the yelp and struggle it elicited.

"Ha, ha, gotcha good, didn't I?" Hank howled with glee.

The dog tried to growl and snap, which angered Hank, so he placed his arm across the dog's head and held one front paw with his hand. The knife cut into the soft pad of the pup's paw with marked precision. The growl quickly morphed into cries of agony.

Hank felt a tightening at his waist. He ignored the sensation and focused on torturing his defenseless captive. He coughed as the tightness squeezed his midsection, taking away his breath. He dropped the knife, feeling around for the cause of his discomfort. His belt grew tighter against his stomach. Hank fumbled with the shiny buckle, trying to release it, but it wouldn't budge. He tried to move it from side to side, up and down, but it held firm, tightening yet another notch and then another. Hank fell to his side as the belt dug deeper into his body. It crushed his intestines seconds before his kidneys burst. His eyes met those of the tormented pup as the last bit of air was squeezed from Hank's lungs.

The pup sniffed, smelling death. He guardedly rose to four feet. His paw ached from the deep cut and it left a trail of blood when he approached the human form. He sniffed the length of the body and cautiously nuzzled the head. The man did not move. A new scent flooded into the pup's awareness: the smell of fresh meat.

***

Where in hell is Hank? He's never late. In fact, Hank always arrived five minutes before clock-in time. Which had been two hours ago and Fred was beginning to worry. He pulled up Hank's phone number from the computer's employee records, pushed the numbers on the phone pad, and listened. After seven rings, his call went to voice mail. Fred decided to stop by Hank's place on his way to investigate an animal abuse call. It was only a few blocks out of his way.

***

Fred rang the bell and listened for footsteps. After a few minutes, he rang the bell again and added a knock on the door.
"Hey, Hank, it's Fred. Are you in there?"
He waited a few more minutes, then tried the doorknob. The door opened and Fred walked into the living room.
"Hank? Hank? Where are you, partner?"
He could hear a low growl coming from somewhere. Fred walked into the kitchen and saw the basement door was open. Fred rushed down the stairs and saw a small dog chewing on something, but he couldn't quite make out what it was in the dim light. Fred walked closer to the cage. It took a minute for what he was seeing to register, and a minute longer before he could stop gagging long enough to pull out his phone and call the authorities.

***

It was one of the strangest cases she'd ever heard of. Emily couldn't imagine one of their own team torturing poor animals, never mind getting away with it. How had no one known for so many years?
She looked down at the pup, whose furry coat was clean and shiny. His eyes were bright and clear and the cuts to his body had almost completely healed. Looking at him now, she couldn't imagine this sweet little pup eating the flesh of a man. They'd quarantined him until the vet gave him a clean bill of health. Now she had the happy task of returning him to his home.
The twenty-minute drive passed quickly. She slowed the car and looked out the window, seeking an address. There it was. She turned her vehicle left into the driveway.
A squealing young girl came to the car before she could even get out.

The Wheel's Final Turn

"Wow, honey, slow down. We'll have your doggy to you in a minute." Emily lifted the carrier out from the passenger seat.

"Let's get him in the house, why don't we, before we let him out," suggested Emily to the child.

Jennifer followed Emily up the porch and opened the door. Her mother was waiting and led the way to the kitchen where Emily set the animal carrier on the linoleum floor. When she released the latch, the pup raced out and he jumped into Jennifer's arms. Jennifer giggled and held him close.

The blackness lurked outside the door and cringed. It vowed to never fail again.

Chapter Twenty-eight
Show Time at the Oracle

"Elaine, did you see my blue denim shirt?"

Jared's knew his nerves were kicking in. Even though the rehearsal had gone so well the other day, this was a huge undertaking. Not only was his artistic life on the line, so was his political career. It was a lot of pressure.

"Here you go, handsome." Elaine tossed the shirt playfully in his direction. He caught it with ease. Jared looked at his wife in amazement. God, she was beautiful.

Elaine held her tresses to the top of her head. "Should I wear my hair up or down?" She removed her hands, letting her rich auburn hair fall to her shoulders. She flashed Jared a smile, well aware which he preferred. Jared returned the smile and pointed down.

The ring of his cell phone interrupted their brief interlude. He picked it up from the end table and hit answer. "Hello."

"Hi, Jared. How are you doing?"

He immediately recognized the voice of Sandra McBride. "A case of the jitters is setting in. But guess that should be expected. After all, I'm putting my reputation on the line. So what's up?" He checked his hair in the full-length mirror, unzipped his pants and tucked the royal blue shirttails inside. After zipping up the jeans, he began to pace.

"Now, don't get upset. Rumor has it Stanley Morris will be attending the concert."

Jared grimaced. He despised that sorry excuse for a reporter. The guy was bad news. His media coverage was pure sensationalism. He'd take an adversarial position on just about any issue, not caring what was important to the public, just so it sold papers and made headlines.

"Thanks for letting me know, Sandra. I can handle that jerk. Hey, after all, he's got to like music."

"Let's hope he likes *your* music, Jared, or he'll try to make you the laughing stock of the political world. Well, off to get ready for the onslaught of press. I'll see you at the coliseum shortly. Bye, Governor."

"Goodbye, Sandra." He picked up the white denim jacket lying on the bed and tucked the phone into the left pocket before putting his arms into the sleeves. He turned and looked into the mirror again. A piece of hair was sticking up from the back of his head. Wetting his forefinger, he slicked it into place.

"Not bad for a middle-aged old fart," Elaine teased from across the room. "Are you about ready to hit the road? It's almost show time."

"I'll check and see if the car's here yet. Be right back. Will you grab Blue for me, hon? The guitar case in the closet?"

One of the benefits of being governor was the chauffer-driven limo and full security. He felt fortunate to have a well-mannered, professional driver named James Everly. They had even become friends over the last few months. James was always willing to listen to Jared's thoughts and ideas. Plus he played a mean sax.

As Elaine opened the closet door, she felt an icy chill run through her body, as if an ominous presence had somehow hidden inside. The air suddenly felt a bit heavy and there seemed to be a grayish tint to it. She felt uneasy, like someone was watching her. She heard Jared call from downstairs, "Elaine, it's time to get going."

"Be right there," she answered. She picked up the guitar case and closed the closet door, feeling relief at being able to leave the hostile space. She grabbed her small purse and hurried down to join Jared. After locking the front door, they hurried to the waiting limousine. The chauffeur had the door open. Jared handed him the guitar case, saying, "Take good care of this one, it's my baby." The chauffeur nodded. "Sure thing, Governor Williams."

Once inside the roomy back seat, the door closed, they were unobservable, and Elaine began to relax.

Once James had settled back into the driver's seat, Jared looked straight at him and ordered, "Let's get going, James. It's show time." All three laughed, and Elaine felt her mood lighten.

The darkness crept silently into the minute gaps between the limousine doors and windows. Hidden from the naked eye, it concealed itself by settling underneath Elaine and Jared's seat, remaining still and soundless, anticipating the moment when it would reveal itself to the masses.

The limo driver pulled into the Oracle Coliseum's massive parking lot, pulled up next to the curb in front of the V.I.P entrance, and waited until the attendant arrived to open the door for Elaine and Jared. They exited the vehicle and the limo pulled away. Security surrounded the couple as they were whisked inside to the entertainers' room. Jared scanned the area for Sandra and saw her sitting at the far end of the room speaking to the stage manager, Mike Garber, who, seeing Jared, excused himself.

"Welcome to the funny farm, Jared. Glad to see our main attraction made it. And who is this lovely lady?" Mike gave Elaine a quick smile and a mischievous wink.

"Hands off, Mike. This is my wife and I aim to keep it that way." Jared chuckled. He'd often seen that appreciative look in men's eyes when they met Elaine.

"Mike, I'll catch you later. I need to get the wife situated and meet with Ms. McBride."

Mike gave a thumbs up. "Got it, Gov."

Elaine decided to mingle with the other political wives and allow Jared to prepare for his performance. After giving him a kiss on the lips, she said, "Well, off I go to spend some time with those boring, gossipy wives. You owe me one for this." Jared frowned. She straightened the collar of his white denim jacket and said, "Make me proud, sweetheart. Show them what Jared Williams is made of."

He winked. "You got it baby."

***

He sat in the center seat in the back row of the arena, anxious, growing restless. He hoped he had performed the mission correctly. He might be good at whittlin', but electronics was another matter. Jest would have to wait and see. Only time would tell. Yup, only time would tell.

***

The lights flashed off and on to signal that first speaker would be coming on stage. The crowd's roar hushed to silence as the stage lit up. A man dressed in a business suit walked to the microphone sitting down center stage.

"Good evening, my fine friends and welcome to the first ever musical performance and speaking engagement created for our own governor, Jared Williams."

The crowd applauded and cheered.

"My name is Victor English, and I've been working with this fine man for several years. Funny thing is, I didn't know he had hidden talent as a musician and singer. You can bet I'm looking forward to his performance today."

Most of the people in the crowd laughed.

"Before we bring out Governor Williams, I believe one of his staff member has a few words to say on his behalf, so let's give a big round of applause for Ms. Sandra McBride."

The spotlight followed Sandra from the side of the stage to down stage center. She whispered into Victor's ear. They shook hands and Victor left the stage. Sandra scanned the audience before speaking into the microphone.

"Well, well, well. Seems I'm not the only fan of Governor Williams. It's nice to see so many supporters with us"

The crowd applauded in response.

Sandra lowered her voice a bit and continued, "We're pleased to bring you another side of politics, the personal side, the private side, the side most people never get to see. I personally want to thank Jared Williams for opening his private life to you."

Another loud round of applause filled the air.

Sandra's voice rose again. "You, all of you here, will be the first to see this one of his many talents." As she spoke the next words, she moved from front left to front right stage, her voice rising to almost a shout. "All we ask in return is for your support come Election Day. If you like what you see, if you believe in all our great governor has done for the State of California, then get out and vote. We cannot keep on the right course without your help."

The audience clapped with enthusiasm.

She lowered her voice to almost a whisper. "We need you, the governor needs you, and the state and country needs you. Now, our grand governor, Jared Williams."

The audience rose from their seats, giving both her and Jared a standing ovation.

The stage lights were bumped up to full capacity as Jared and the rest of the performers took their places.

Jared stood before the microphone. "California, are you ready to rock!" The crowd erupted with cheers and applause. He strummed the first few chords of the music before the band joined him and began his song.

"Every man and woman, each awakening mind, needs a bit of courage to really change the times.

Some call me a dreamer. Some say I'm a sham. Listen to me people, I'm only what I am, an honest man."

Jared continued his performance and the audience adored him. They raised their arms to the sky, danced in the aisles and in their seats. They were buying his propaganda as if it were gospel.

Sweat poured from Jared's brow. His clothing was soaked. The band broke into five minutes of instrumental as Jared introduced each member and the spotlight focused on them as they played. Jared wiped his forehead with a clean white towel and tossed it to the side.

"Let's not forget our lovely ladies, the best backup singers in the industry."

The audience went wild when the young women broke into a harmonic verse. Jared exited the stage, but he could hear the mantra, "Jared, Jared," repeated by the crowd. He allowed a few minutes of time to pass and the plea grew louder. "Jared, Jared."

He walked back on stage and the audience stood for another ovation.

Jared walked to the microphone. The stage lights dimmed and the crowd grew silent.

The gray-haired man pushed the button.

Governor Williams' fingers touched the strings of Blue and he strummed a chord. Bolts of electricity surged from the strings and into Jared's body. His body twitched and he fell to the hard wooden stage floor in convulsions. The crowd gasped in shock and several people began to scream. Elaine gasped and ran up the stairs to the right of the stage, hurrying to her husband's side. The stage went black as the on-the-scene paramedics rushed in. Aside from charred hands and a slightly elevated heartrate, they decreed him well enough to be transported to the hospital.

Elaine heard its mocking laughter. She'd also seen darkness surround her husband's body while he lay on the stage floor. At first, it floated above him, then, to her surprise, she saw it enter his injured body. Elaine didn't know what to do. Nobody would believe such a story.

The words came to her in a melodious vibration of spirit and purity of air.

Elaine, he must be removed from his bed. He is not safe where he lays. The violence of history, the cruelty of humankind, the hatred of brother, the emptiness of soul is within this man.

She understood the words referred to Jared. Not knowing why, she recognized the melody. Without warning, if in a trance, her hand grabbed a pen from her purse, a paper from her wallet, and she began writing. The words told their own tale. As suddenly as it had begun, it ceased, and her senses returned. The paper fell from her hand; and she snatched it before it landed on the ground.

Elaine read the words written in unfamiliar handwriting: Take your husband to Guadalupe Park in San Jose. He will be safe there.

A feeling of comfort came over her and blanketed her soul with love and her mind with knowledge. "Yes," Elaine thought, "the park." She raced to the limousine and pulled the door open before James had the opportunity.

"Get in, James. Hurry. We're going to Kaiser Permanente Hospital. Hurry."

A bitter, foul odor trailed into the vehicle with her. The darkness was ready to fight.

Chapter Twenty-nine
A Father's Love

Much as she hated to admit it, Alana had looked beautiful and she'd handled the questions and the crowd with ease. It sure would have been easier on her ego if her replacement had stumbled or lost her composure. But it was over, that chapter of that part of her life. She was ready to start anew. Now she just had to figure out what and where.

Misty's stomach growled, a reminder that she hadn't eaten since morning. She kicked off her heels and padded to the kitchen. Her cat jumped from the top of the refrigerator and welcomed her with a sweet meow. She bent over and petted her from head to tail. "Bet you're hungry, too." As if she understood, the cat answered with another meow.

Misty removed a can of sardines from the cabinet, retrieved a fork from the utensil drawer, and scooped out three large sardines into the cat bowl on the floor. Needing no coaching, her feline companion settled in to enjoy the treat. When Misty attempted to pet her, the cat growled softly while still munching its food. "Okay, baby, Mama won't bother you while you're eating." She'd only done it because it worked every time, and the growls always made her laugh.

Then she heard another sound, a voice. When Misty ignored it, the voice became louder.

Be not afraid. I am here to help you.

Now she was getting frightened. She grabbed a butcher knife from the wooden block on the counter and circled the room, holding the large knife up with her right hand.

"Where are you? I have a knife."

Angelic, light laughter floated through her mind.

Your knife is useless against me. I mean you no harm. I am here to ask your help.

"Okay," Misty said, "I'll play. What kind of help? I don't even know who you are. Why would I want to help you?"

I know you don't believe me though all I say is truth. I know no other than certainty. Within the world grows a darkness, an evil. It grows larger and more powerful each moment. If we do nothing, it will control the souls and minds of all the creatures of the earth. Ultimately, it will destroy the world.

"Yeah, right. I hear some voice, probably my imagination, and I'm supposed to believe it's real. No way."

An orb of light appeared before her. It floated and bounced through the air and grew larger in size until she saw the form of a man standing in front of her. Misty squinted her eyes, looked away and then back again, knowing it would be gone. To her amazement, it was still there and had solidified to form the body of her father. She gasped in both fear and attraction. She loved her father. He had died when she was sixteen years old. She'd give anything to speak with him one more time.

"Daddy, is it really you?"

The figure answered, not in words, but in thoughts projected clearly into her mind

Yes, Pumpkin Face, it is me. I have little time to spend with you. I vibrate on a different frequency and my energy is limited. Misty, you must believe me and heed my words. They are important.

She knew this was her father. No one else ever called her "Pumpkin Face." In fact, she'd forgotten the nickname years ago.

"I will, Daddy, I promise. What is it that is so important?"

When the time is right, you will go to San Jose Guadalupe Park. There you will find three other people. You will know who they are because I will be there to guide you. One is named Angela. You must protect her. Listen to what she tells you and follow her instructions.

"Okay, but when? How will I know the right time?"

Misty, my dearest daughter, when I return, it will be time.

"But, Daddy—"

The being had vanished.

Chapter Thirty
Like Mother, Like Daughter

As she looked through the slightly ajar bedroom door, she could feel the darkness around her. It had entered her home and focused on Monty's weaknesses. The last time she'd checked on him, he'd been rambling about his childhood. That damn darkness had found his sore spot again. Angela had tried to relieve his distress by bringing him some fresh fruit, but he insisted on cake or cookies. In his mind, he was still a fat, shy, lonely kid. He didn't even recognize her. Monty was lost in his delirium.

"Mommy, can I talk to you?"

Angela shut the bedroom door and turned to her daughter, startled by the look of fear on Alicia's face.

"Sweetie, what's going on?"

"I'm afraid to go to sleep. Something's in the bedroom." Alicia's brow furrowed and her lips quivered as she threw her arms around her mother's waist and held on tightly.

Oh, no, not my child, too. Angela put her arm around her daughter's shoulder. "Tell me, what's in your bedroom? What does it look like?"

"It doesn't look like anything. It is just black. And, Mommy, what scares me most is it wants to touch me."

"Does Alexis see it?"

Alicia shrugged her shoulders. "She says she doesn't see it and makes fun of me. So I don't mention it to her anymore. You believe me, Mommy, don't you?"

Angela removed Alicia's arms from around her waist and crouched down so they were face to face. "Of course I believe you, sweetie. Mommy sees it, too. I think it is time you and I had a talk. Come on, let's go downstairs into the kitchen and we'll figure this out together, okay?"

Alicia followed her mother down the stairs and into the kitchen. She took a seat at the kitchen table and watched as Angela removed a pitcher of iced tea from the refrigerator. Alicia popped out of her seat and went to the cabinet to remove two silver-rimmed drinking glasses. She handed them to her mother who pressed each glass against the ice dispenser and filled them half full of crushed ice. Angela set one glass in front of her daughter, who had returned to her seat. She walked around the table, pulled the chair out and sat before setting her own glass down.

"May I pour the tea, Mommy?"

"Sure thing, kiddo," Angela handed the pitcher to her daughter. "So tell me when you first noticed this odd stuff."

As she poured the tea into her mother's glass, Alicia replied. "How do I know what's odd if it isn't odd to me? I mean, what if these things happen all the time? Is that odd then?"

Amazing what a smart kid Monty and I made. "You've got me on that one," she said with a grin. "But let me tell you a secret. From what you're telling me, I should have told you long ago. I have seen these things ever since I was a little girl. Just like you."

Alicia's eyes brightened. "You have? You mean I'm not stupid like Alexis says?"

Angela's heart went out to her daughter. She knew the feeling of being 'different', of people not believing you, and of being afraid to tell the truth.

"You are *not* stupid. Though the honest truth is, Alicia, you *are* different from many other people. But not in a bad way, sweetie. You, like me, have a precious gift. Most people don't understand it. Ever hear the saying, what we don't know, we fear? Guess folks would need to experience it to truly understand it."

Her mother's words seemed to lift her spirit and Alicia smiled.

"You know, Mother, maybe we *are* special. Maybe God picked us out over everybody else."

"Oh, everyone is special, honey. Each of us has our own unique gifts to bring into the world. Our gift just happens to be the ability to see beyond the physical world and into the spiritual. Do you understand?"

Alicia thought for a moment. She took another gulp of tea and set the glass on the table. "Is spirit bad, Mother?"

Angela laughed. "Oh, my goodness, no. Spirit is within all of us. It's what we began as before we were born and what we end up as after we die. It is beautiful."

Alicia pondered her mother's words, trying to understand their meaning. "So we see and talk to people before they're born and after they die?"

"You got it. Right on the nose." Angela stretched across the table and gave her daughter's nose a tweak. She was rewarded with a giggle.

"Okay, enough of this, baby. Just promise me if you're ever afraid, you'll come to me. It can be our own little secret."

Alicia ran to give her mother a relieved hug. She drew away and started walking toward the living room, then came back and asked, "What about the darkness? It scares me."

"If ever the darkness comes, I want you to think about love, nothing else. Think only about love. Can you do that, baby?"

"Of course I can think about love. Duh. That's easy."

Angela ruffled Alicia's hair and playfully smacked her on the rear

The Wheel's Final Turn

end.

"Well, duh, I was only asking," she teased back.

She watched her daughter settle onto the sofa and click on the TV.

***

It's time. You must call Euclid and Karman. The words were soft yet firmly stated.

"No", her soul cried. "Not now," she said aloud.

Over these things, we have no control. If not now, when? When it is too late for mankind? When the world has been destroyed? Is this what you wish, Angela?

"Okay, what must I do?"

I will guide your hand and sit beside you. For now, you are to tell Euclid and Karman to be at the Guadalupe Park in San Jose. They will know when, as will you. Remember, you will be joined by a woman; you will be a circle of four. This is most important.

Angela knew by the stillness of the air that it was gone. She picked up the cell phone from the kitchen counter and dialed. Voice mail. She seemed to have the worst timing. All she could do was hope they'd get her message quickly.

"It's Angela, guys. Look, I need you to meet me at Guadalupe Park in San Jose, near the Children's Discovery Museum. You'll know when the time is right." Her voice softened and lowered in decibel. "Look, just be there, okay?"

She had one last thing left to do before she left. Perhaps the most important of all. Angela rushed up the stairs to Monty's side.

"Get up," she ordered, her voice forceful.

Monty did not stir.

Angela placed her hands on his shoulders and shook him with all her might. "I said, get up."

Still he did not move.

Angela pulled her hand back and swung, slapping him across the face. He stirred, mumbled an incoherent word or two, and raised his upper body off the bed. He looked at his wife. Her face was filled with anger.

"You get dressed right now. I don't care how long it takes, but you get dressed and get your ass to Guadalupe Park. You know where it is, near the downtown convention center. Monty, listen to me. If we have any chance at all of fighting this darkness, you *must* do as I say."

Monty heard the music of angels playing a harmonious song. It urged him to his feet.

Angela heard the music and no longer feared for Monty. It would show him the way.

***

Before leaving for the park, Angela went to the twins' room. She picked up Old Teddy from the dresser and cuddled him next to her breast. It had been on Alexis's third birthday that she'd gifted her daughter with the bear. Alicia'd gotten the bunny. She wondered what happened to Bunny Bun. She'd have to search the moving boxes in the attic. It didn't seem right, Old Teddy without Bunny Bun. Yes, she would do that tomorrow.

Alexis stirred and woke. "Mom?"

Angela put her forefinger to her mouth. "Shush, Alex. Let Alicia sleep." She sat on the bed and gave Alexis a hug and kiss. "Now get some rest, baby."

Drowsy, Alexis lay back, closed her eyes, and was soon fast asleep.

Angela moved near Alicia's bed. She didn't wish to wake her, so opted to just blow her a kiss.

She walked down the stairway and into the bathroom, opened the vanity drawer and rumbled through it. Finding the elastic band, she pulled her blonde hair off her face and pulled it back into a ponytail. She slipped on the white canvas mules she'd earlier left in the room and walked to the hallway. Her keys hung from the board Monty had built especially for her. Her eyes went to the small heart he had engraved in the upper left corner and it melted her own. Angela removed the keychain from its metal holder. She turned, opened the entranceway door and stepped outside.

Okay. Now I'm ready to fight.

Chapter Thirty-one
The Wheel's Final Turn

Angela parked her car in the closest lot to the Guadalupe River Park in downtown San Jose. She hoped Euclid and Karman had received her voice mail. There was little time to spare. She exited the vehicle, shut the door, and instinctively hit her key ring, locking the vehicle securely.

As she walked toward the northeast side of the park's entrance, the wind grew even more violent, forcing her to clutch her purse to her chest for fear it would be torn from her shoulder. Even with the weather conditions, as she walked down the concrete path she had to appreciate the magnificently landscaped grounds. Lush green grass grew beneath a variety of trees. She noticed an old California Pepper tree and feared it would uproot from the force of the wind. The contrast between metal, wood, and concrete architecture amid the well-kept landscape was art in itself.

She looked for her friends and saw them standing next to a large grove of Pistachio trees in the Aids Memorial Grove near the Children's Discovery building. Angela waved and felt relieved when they waved back.

She rushed to them and embraced each one individually, feeling their hearts' rapid beats against her breast. Adrenalin surged through her body and she said a silent prayer for strength and unfaltering focus. They had to stay centered and purposeful.

Angela released herself from Karman's embrace, and stepped back with arms outstretched, hands firmly gripping her friend's shoulders.

"Thank God you came."

The wind howled through the trees and the air became dense and foreboding. They could hear the screams of anguish, anger, and hatred from the crowd that had gathered in the streets, unbearably loud and growing in intensity. Blackness hid the sunlight with its dusty ebony and gray color. The cries of the crowd echoed into the darkness that consumed each plea of despair with pleasure, bouncing it back into the atmosphere with extreme force, doubling, tripling, and quadrupling its effect upon minds and souls.

Euclid reached out and caught Angela as she teetered from the pressure of the darkness's force. She drew several gasps of air into her lungs, each tasting of oily, defecated refuse.

"Steady there, girl."

She recovered her footing and took his hands as she lowered herself to the ground.

Alarmed, Karman ran to Angela's side. "You cannot do this, Ang. You're too exhausted. Let Euclid and me handle it."

Angela looked into Karman's face and, with a labored breath, said, "No. It must be us three, and one other. Whoever that person should be, we have been told they will come and we shall welcome them enthusiastically. Besides, Karman, you know it wants me. I must be part of this or it will never end."

"Whatever you say, Angela. But I don't like it. I don't like this one bit."

Angela turned her head and saw Wayne, Jared, Alana, and Monty approaching, zombie-like, with blank stares, slow movements, and hollow eyes. Yet she sensed some goodness deep within their souls, and she did not fear their nearing.

A young woman walked up to Euclid. Her purple sundress blew into her face and she pushed it down and held it to her legs. A look of recognition flashed between them.

"Mister, I don't know why, but I've been told to come to this place at this very moment. Know this sounds mad, but I've been sent by powers stronger than I who said you'd understand."

He recognized her immediately. She was the woman from the media event with Alana. So she was the person they'd been foretold, the fourth.

"Happy to see ya, uh, didn't catch the name."

"My name's Misty Lane and I'm here to help. What can I do?"

Angela's eyes glowed with peace as she looked upon the newcomer. Yes, she was the fourth indeed, the perfect completion of their circle. She turned to the raven-haired young woman. "First of all, Misty Lane, you are *not* crazy. You have a very important role to undertake today."

"Yes, I was told so. How can I help?"

"I'll lead and you can follow us. First, sit down and we'll form a circle in front of the Pistachio trees."

Euclid, Karman, Misty, and Angela sat upon the green grass, the trees intertwined before them, and reached out their arms and joined hands.

"What do we do now?" Misty inquired.

With a glow on her face, Angela whispered, "We pray."

Her voice filled the air with the sweetness of honey, the tenderness of loving kisses, and the tone of angels.

"Dear God, our Father, our Mother, our Creator, we sit humbly before you, mere mortals of flesh and bone, with grace and obedience of the laws of the earth and heavens. We plead to you, we beg you to accept our love so pure and our goodness so precious. We ask that you shelter us from the darkness of the world and protect us from the blackness of the universe which has grown more malevolent each minute of every day."

The wind shifted direction and slammed into Angela with such vehemence that Karman and Euclid were forced to tighten their grips on her hands. The blackness descended, forming a circle that surrounded and caged the four. It inched its way under their arms, between their fingers, and filled the entire area they occupied with a scent that became almost unbearable, as though the remains of corpses from all the years before and the centuries to come had channeled into one putrid odor.

Karman shook her head and closed her eyes as the wind stung her face and the rank smell filled her nose. She gagged, making it worse by taking more of the despicable smell into her mouth, and suppressed the urge to vomit, pushing the acidy contents down her throat.

Euclid sat still, his eyes closed, and his mind centered on love, peace, and goodness. The wind roared in his ears and bits of twigs hit his wrinkled face, yet he remained calm, lost in meditation, concentrating on the Universe and Its grace and love.

Angela looked directly into Misty's eyes,

"We must *all* close our eyes and think of nothing but love. No matter what is going on around us, it is meaningless and powerless against the worship of love. Love is eternal and all-powerful. This we must do without hesitation or reservation. This we must do with intent and conviction."

The four chosen ones held their ground and, with closed eyes, meditated solely on love. As they did so, the glow that had first appeared on Angela's face grew in intensity and spread, still emanating from her, until it fully encompassed the circle.

Alana, Wayne, Jared, and Monty stood behind them, hands joined. Tears streamed from their eyes, and their skin was ripped and bleeding from debris hurled at their now half-naked bodies. Alana, once the picture of physical beauty, was so no longer. Her head was bald and shining in the brilliance of the light surrounding the four. Her once silky, soft skin was covered with oozing blisters from head to toe, and her clothes were ragged and torn. She looked nothing like her former self.

Wayne, Jared, and Monty had no obvious physical imperfections, but they had been much easier for the darkness to control than Alana. It hadn't taken much effort for the malevolence to take over their souls and ravage their minds. The wickedness of their past deeds required little coaxing in order to be revealed once again. The blackness knew it would soon have their hearts.

Still, they were vigilant as they stared at the four figures in front of them, focusing only on the radiance of the light. Their hearts guided them against the pull of darkness. All they could see, sense, or comprehend was the glow emitting from Angela's body. It mesmerized them.

"This is your salvation."

Rain poured from the darkness in razor sharp drops onto the land and the people. It cut into their eyes and sliced their bodies. The air filled with screams of pain. Several people lay on the ground, writhing in torment, while others repeatedly vomited until there was nothing left but the urge. Their breathing was labored. There was no escape from the wickedness.

A roar of guttural laughter bellowed from above and traveled around and into the souls of each man, woman, and child. It mocked their fragility and weakness, and turned into a deafening chant of "Retsasid, retsasid, retsasid," never faltering, piercing their ears with its intense volume.

Still they sat, the four, meditating as Alana, Wayne, Jared, and Monty looked on.

Angela began chanting, "Oh, Father/Mother, Creator of All, blanket us with protection against the darkness. Fill our hearts and souls with your eternal love. Strengthen our bodies with the will to survive, the power to fight."

The four were in unison, repeating the mantra; their voices grew in volume until the words were louder than the sound of the thunderous darkness. Lightning struck the Children's Discovery building, sending sparks into the sky. Another bolt hit one of the Pistachio trees, splitting its limbs. Tendrils of gray smoke rose from the tree.

The thunder grew louder, further feeding the darkness that developed rapidly and stretched its mass to encompass cities and towns, then whole states, spreading through the United States and outward around the world. From China to the Middle East, from England to Antarctica, its hungry thirst for vengeance against good quickly overcame the souls of men. "Retsasid" echoed across each land and into each mind, causing ears to bleed from its unbearable powerful volume. Kings, presidents, and elected officials, brought to their knees, were unable to fight or stop the blackness of centuries from its ugly path of destruction. No military weapon or scientific instrument could penetrate or destroy it. The end seemed inevitable. Thousands rushed, limped or crawled to churches, synagogues, mosques, temples, and altars, praying and chanting to their specific deities. The world was united in disaster and. simultaneously, in prayer.

The four's voices grew clearer, louder, filled the air and rose into the heavens of the sky until they became one, spreading over the earth. It was magical. The tone was vociferous enough to challenge the voice of the darkness, yet, at the same time, it bore the sweetness of angels as the harmony continued its valiant fight.

The light emitting from Angela grew, jutting out and cutting through the dark dense space. The shining light of love expanded. It reached into the sky and traveled around the world, creating large gaps of brightness within the massive dark. The blackness howled, unwilling to give in to love. With survival as its overriding concern, it concentrated itself into an enormous ball and focused on the light's source of power.

Angela's body jerked in response to a direct hit from the darkness. Relentlessly, it attacked her small body. She cried out in agony, still holding tightly to Euclid's and Karman's hands.

"Angela, no! This must stop," cried Euclid, letting go of her firm grasp.

Karman and Misty followed suit and released their hold of one another. They stood and looked on in horror as the unrelenting force of evil rammed into Angela's unyielding body. Again and again it attacked, bruising her body, shearing her soft skin.

Misty could stand it no longer. "Stop," she cried. "Leave her be. Take me instead."

Thunder roared above her, contemptuous and mocking. Lightning bolts flew through the sky. She didn't know what to do. She felt helpless in the face of the phenomenon.

Alana screamed in horror as the ball of darkness, increasing its power, directing itself, once again into Angela's battered body.

With a will of strength he didn't know he possessed, Monty flung off the grasp of the darkness and ran to Angela's side. He was instantly shoved backward, his body hurled into the air. He landed on the concrete pavement; one leg lay upward, broken.

Wayne, also now awake, ran to Monty's side. He looked into Monty's anguished face and cupped it in his hands. They shared a moment of acknowledgment that they were powerless to fight the force.

Gold and white rays of light filled the skies as Angela and the others continued their chant of eternal love, vibrating and sending energy and lightness throughout the world.

"Chant these words with me, please," Angela begged in labored voice. "I cannot do this alone."

Euclid said, "She is right, ya know. One way or the other, we must finish this."

"Love is eternal. Love is grace. May the goodness of Love live within the hearts of mankind."

Their words echoed, sending reverberations throughout the world, reaching far into the heavens, traveling to every country, reaching each person's ears. Feeling the miracle, the people all over the planet began to chant the mantra. Their united voices reached into eternity. The earth beneath them vibrated and the sky lit up and sparkled upon hearing the wishes of man.

Anger at its defeat surged through the darkness. It would not give up that easily. The source was all that mattered, so it enveloped Angela's body, entering into each pore. It squeezed her heart and collapsed her lungs. She screeched in agony, then gasped one last time before collapsing into the arms of death.

Karman turned Angela onto her back. She placed her right hand on Angela's breastbone and laid the other atop it. One, two, three, four, five, she silently counted until she had reached the recommended thirty compressions. Getting no result, she blew two puffs of air into her friend's shredded lungs and continued the compressions, unable to see through her tears.

The blackness laughed in deafening glee, confident it had regained control.

Euclid released his grip on Misty's hand. He rose and went behind his wife and placed his large hands upon her shoulders. He looked down at Angela's lifeless body.

"She's gone, Karman. You kin stop now," he said in a voice that didn't even try to hide his heartbreak.

Karman shook her head. "No, I can't Euclid, never. I can't let her go."

Euclid removed Karman's hands from Angela's chest. He knelt beside her, took her into his arms, and they sought comfort when there was none to be found.

Monty sobbed loudly, overcome with grief and loss.

Jared was outraged. Then something clicked. It was a thought so obvious he couldn't believe he hadn't figured it out already. "People, listen. We must continue the chant. Do not stop now or it will mean disaster. You hear me? Disaster. Don't you get it? Retsasid is disaster spelled in reverse."

Jared sat down next to Angela's lifeless body and reached his arms out to Euclid and Karman. Through tears of grief, they accepted his hand in theirs and once again sat upon the lush green grass. Misty, Alana, Wayne, and Monty soon joined them.

Into the silence came a wondrous choir of chanting.

"Surround us with love. Protect us from darkness. Deliver us from this evil."

As before, the mantra traveled through space and time, sending its message throughout the world.

The sky opened. The faces of Jesus, Buddha, Mohammad, Confucius, the visages of all the gods known and unknown from the beginning of time filled the heavens. They twirled and spun in a glorious dance of harmony until they joined as one gigantic, pulsating, radiant circle. The sphere of light descended upon the darkness with unrelenting intent. It sucked in the thunder, lightning, and ravishing wind, turning them to

The Wheel's Final Turn

brilliant rays of warm sunshine. The darkness whimpered as, its power removed, it floated helplessly amid the light's illumination. It cried in anguish as the light exhaled universal love into its being. The blackness burst and splintered outward until it was drawn into and became part of the light, no longer able to use its power against the earth.

All that remained was the omnipotence of Spirit, the presence of love.

From the circle of gods two hands reached down and drew the body of Angela upward, holding her against the brightness of the light for the entire world to see. People everywhere stood in awe as they observed the miracle.

Angela's body awakened from death's grip as she was held suspended above the earth. She looked upon the people of the world. Purple, blue, gold and white light surrounded her, so brilliant it lit up the entire sky. She smiled, letting them know she was not only at peace, but also at home. Her smile touched their souls, warmed their hearts, and dissolved all fear. After one final nod, Angela disappeared into the light.

Where it was night, the stars twinkled bright; where it was day, the sky shined with sunlight through blue sky.

The people now united as one, knowing all gods were One, and that each man's fate was his brother's.

Creator smiled.

And in the end, the love you take is equal to the love you make
From "The End" Composed by Paul McCartney
(although credited to John Lennon)

About the Author

A member of The Missouri Writers Guild, Writers Center and former columnist for Authors Info, Monica's articles and stories can be found in TheWriteroomblog, A Word With You Press, Broowaha, and All Voices, among other places.

The highly rated reviews of her first novel, *The Turn of the Karmic Wheel*, prove that readers embrace both her creativity and unique story line.

Along with writing, Monica co-hosts a weekly internet, on-camera radio show, It Matters Radio. Each broadcast showcases talented musical artists as well as authors, non-profit organizations, political/news figures or celebrities. "If we find something important and meaningful, we will bring it to our listeners."

Viewers say her hearty laughter fills the air, and, friends say, warms their hearts.

A former director, singer, and actress, Monica spends her time, when not writing, assisting new talent gain exposure.

She lives in Missouri with her husband, five cats, and two dogs.
Visit her web sites:
On The Brink: http://itmattersradio.wix.com/on-the-brink
A Touch of Karma: http://theturnofthekarmicwheel.blogspot.com/
It Matters Radio: www.itmattersradio.com

ALL THINGS THAT MATTER PRESS

FOR MORE INFORMATION ON TITLES AVAILABLE FROM
ALL THINGS THAT MATTER PRESS, GO TO
http://allthingsthatmatterpress.com
or contact us at
allthingsthatmatterpress@gmail.com

Made in United States
Orlando, FL
28 March 2023